Full Figured 2:

Carl Weber Presents

Full Figured 2:

Carl Weber Presents

By Alexis Nicole and Trista Russell

URBAN
Renaissance

www.urbanbooks.net

Urban Books, LLC
78 East Industry Court
Deer Park, NY 11729

ISBN 13: 978-1-60162-231-0
ISBN 10: 1-60162-231-7

First Printing November 2010
Printed in the United States of America

10 9 8 7 6 5 4 3 2 1

*This is a work of fiction. Any references or similarities to actual
events, real people, living, or dead, or to real locales are intended to
give the novel a sense of reality. Any similarity in other names, char-
acters, places, and incidents is entirely coincidental.*

Distributed by Kensington Publishing Corp.
Submit Wholesale Orders to:
Kensington Publishing Corp.
C/O Penguin Group (USA) Inc.
Attention: Order Processing
405 Murray Hill Parkway
East Rutherford, NJ 07073-2316
Phone: 1-800-526-0275
Fax: 1-800-227-9604

Back Side of Soul

A Novella

By Alexis Nicole

Chapter 1

I was born to be a star!

It didn't take much for me to imagine myself standing center stage in the middle of Philips Arena. Or maybe the Staples Center in Los Angeles. Or even Madison Square Garden in New York! *That would be sweet.*

I could almost hear myself singing to sold-out crowds, with fans chanting my name: Simone! Simone! Simone!

Just the thought of that made me grin so wide my cheeks hurt.

So, if I was born to be rocking somebody's stage, what was I doing here?

Not that I would ever ask that question out loud. Especially not to anyone here at Greater Faith Baptist Church. No, not a soul would ever hear those words come from my lips, 'cause I'd been raised right. I was a pastor's kid and a daddy's girl. That meant I always did the right thing, especially since I had to pick up the slack from my big sister, Skye. She never did anything right, at least, not in my daddy's eyes. But I was different; I only spoke when I was spoken to, and when I did speak, I only said what everyone expected me to say. So, if I were to tell anyone that I was going to be a star, it would shake up the whole Greater Faith Baptist world.

But just because I didn't say it, didn't mean that it wasn't true.

I was born to be a star!

I felt it the most every time I stood in this choir stand. Here in church, standing behind the organist, and in front of the musical director, singing was all I could think about. I mean, everyone in the choir always said I had the best voice, and though I didn't have a lot of confidence in other areas, I knew that I could sing.

Sometimes, when I was in my dorm room by myself, I would turn up the music so loud the walls would shake, and I would singright along with my girl Yolanda, or Mary Mary. And, sometimes, I even rocked out with Beyonce and Rhianna. Now, it's not like I want to brag, 'cause Daddy says that one who brags is full of pride. But though I understood what my dad meant, sometimes you just have to tell it. And when I sang with Yolanda or Mary Mary or Beyonce or Rhianna, I sounded dang good.

So, if I was so good, why was I here, singing backup for old Miss Maggie?

Okay, that's a bit of an exaggeration—I wasn't really her backup. Miss Maggie was singing the solo, and I was just one of the thirty-six people in the choir, singing behind her.

"This is my story . . ."

I tried not to do it. Tried not to roll my eyes as she held on to that note for as long as she could. In my head, I counted; she held it for five seconds, tops. Now, see, if that had been me, I would've rocked that note for at least double that time.

But no matter how long I could hold a note, or how wide my range was, I was gonna be backup for old Miss Maggie as long as my father was the pastor of Greater Faith.

It was kind of funny that I called Miss Maggie old, since I think she was just something like fifty-seven or fifty-eight; she was around my mom and dad's age and they didn't seem old. But me, Skye, and our girl, Chyanne, had been calling Miss Maggie old since we were little kids. And every time she sang these ancient Negro spirituals, she sounded even older to me.

"This is my song!"

This time, I couldn't help it—I did roll my eyes, even though I tried to keep the smile on my face. But this was so tired, all of it: this song, the way we swayed, Miss Maggie. And I was tired too, of living this life when there was so much more that I wanted to do.

That's when my eyes wandered into the congregation and I looked right into the faces of my two best friends. Chyanne was staring at me with her eyebrows raised so high, they were almost at the top of her forehead. I knew that look. That meant she was about to crack up at any moment. And sitting right next to her was Devin, already laughing, though he had his head down and his hand over his mouth, like he was trying to hide it.

Uh-oh. Chyanne must've seen the look on my face, and we'd been girls for so long, she knew what I was thinking. Or maybe it was Devin who was reading me. I hadn't known Devin as long as Chyanne; Skye and I had known Chyanne since forever and I'd only met Devin in middle school. But that was ten years ago, so he knew what was up just by looking at me.

Well, if my friends had peeped what I was doing, then I needed to straighten up before my daddy or mother saw me. I made sure I didn't turn to the right where my dad was sitting at the altar, dipping his head to the music, and smiling as if he was so proud of his choir. And I certainly didn't look to the left and the first pew where my mom always sat, because if she saw me making faces at old Miss Maggie, my mother just might march right up into this choir stand and snatch me.

So I kept my eyes on Brother Steve, the choir director, and kept my mind away from my dreams.

I sure was glad when Miss Maggie hit that last note and we were finally able to take our seats. Folks were shouting, "Amen!" and "Hallelujah!" and "Thank you, Jesus!"

The smile was still on my face, but not because I was happy about our song or the congregants' reactions; I was just glad that now, if I started daydreaming, no one would be able to see me.

The parishioners were still shouting and my dad sat back; he didn't make a move, as if he wanted to give the folks time to get out all of their praise. I wiggled back in my seat and waited right along with him. One thing was for sure, I knew I would hear a good Word today. That was the thing about my daddy; I hardly ever got bored when he was preaching, because he had a voice that was made for singing. Just listening to him was amazing. And then, he always had a good Word. My dad could break it down so that even the young'uns—as he liked to call us—could understand what he was saying.

Finally, my dad stood and strolled toward the podium. Though my daddy was a preacher, and his daddy was a preacher, and his daddy was a preacher, my dad didn't look anything like a pastor. Back in the day when Skye and I were growing up, we hated when our friends said Daddy looked like a movie star. I mean, it didn't bother me now, but before, when I was little, I didn't want my dad to look special. I just wanted him to look like a daddy.

I had to admit, as I watched him stroll with a swagger that all the guys in church tried to imitate, he did look a little like Idris Elba. But though he had the looks and the strut, my father was sold out for Christ. And he was one of those old-time preachers, seriously old school: girls should wear dresses, only men should preach, and the choir had to sing those tired songs with solos by old women.

Just thinking about how out-of-date my father was made me want to sigh.

"Good morning, saints!"

"Morning, Pastor," rang through the sanctuary.

"You know, I just love that song," he said, turning to look at us in the choir stand.

Okay, I was about to do it again. I was about to roll my eyes.

"Blessed assurance; I know that's right," my father said. "That song is da bomb." He chuckled, as if he'd just said something clever.

See what I mean? Even my dad's slang was old-fashioned. He didn't even know people didn't say "da bomb" anymore.

He kept on. "Y'all better recognize! There is power in the title of that song."

"Preach, Pastor," someone yelled out, though my father had just gotten started.

"We are blessed to have the assurances of God!" my father said, his voice starting to rise. "And here's the thing: we had the assurances of God before, I said, before we were even born!" Now, his voice was booming, bouncing off the huge stainedglass windows. Sometimes when my dad preached, he could make those windows rattle. And he could rattle the people, too.

I looked into the sanctuary and almost shook my head. It didn't take much from my father. He already had the members of Greater Faith going. They were twisting in their seats, lifting their hands, raising their Bibles. And he hadn't said ten sentences.

"How blessed do you have to be to have the Lord's assurances before you were born?" my father asked. "And if you don't believe me, if you don't know that you had His assurances while you were in your mama's womb, let me show you the scripture. Turn to Jeremiah 1:4."

I didn't even wait for my dad to read the words out loud because that just took too long. There were folks who only opened their Bibles on Sundays, and they didn't have any idea whether Jeremiah was in the Old or the New Testament. So sometimes, my father had to wait like, five minutes for everyone to get on the same page.

As soon as I got to the scripture, I read it for myself.

Before I formed you in the womb, I knew you, before you were born,

I set you apart.

Wow! I wondered what the Lord had set me apart to do.

"We were set apart for His blessings," my father said after he read the scripture aloud, "for His assurances, for His grace, and His mercy. Y'all need to hear what I'm saying, saints."

My dad had to pause as people jumped out of their seats and raised their hands and their voices. Most of the time, I couldn't understand a thing these people were saying when they got all happy and holy. When we were kids, this was our favorite part of the service. Skye and I couldn't wait for the old people to start dancing in the aisles and falling out at the altar. We used to crack up, but, now, it just annoyed me sometimes. I'm not saying that people shouldn't get happy, I just couldn't figure out why it was the same people, shouting the same words, and crying the same tears every Sunday.

"Y'all need to know that God wouldn't have tried to know you if He didn't have plans for you," my father said, not letting up. "He wanted to know you because He knew what you would be. He knew how you were going to be as a child, and He knew what you were going to be when you grew up."

Some folks laughed at that, but I didn't. I had never thought of it that way, that God already knew the future. I mean, of course I knew that, but I'd never thought of it in terms of *me.* So, if God knew my future, if He knew what I was going to be when I grew up, I wondered if He thought that I could be a singer.

"So, here's the thing, and y'all need to get these points. We are blessed to have God's assurances. We were blessed before the beginning and we'll be blessed after the end. And we are blessed all the days of our lives in between. No matter what it looks like or feels like, we have His assurances that He wants the best for us. He wants us to reach our goals and have our dreams, as long as they are inside of His will."

Okay, this was deep, because if God wanted me to have my

dream, then I was going to be a singer. But the problem was, that wasn't the way it worked in the Davenport household. Where I lived, Reverend Davenport's dreams were the only ones that counted. And he had always made it very clear what he wanted for me: to go to school and get good grades (which I did). Then, to go to Spelman and major in accounting, because, according to him, that was, practical degree (which I did). And now that I was a senior, he wanted me to graduate with honors (which I was going to do) and go to work for Ernst & Young, where I had interned every summer since my freshman year. That was the part that just made me sigh.

I really needed to stop thinking about this. Because even if my father were to miraculously one day say, "Simone, you should be a singer!" it would still never happen. No matter how good I sounded, no matter how much ambition I had, there was one thing that would always keep me back.

Looking down at the flowing choir robe, I remembered why I was always glad when we wore these on Sundays. Because not only was the golden satin so beautiful, but it hid most of my unflattering curves.

And therein lay the problem. While I may have had the voice that could match anyone on the Billboard Top Ten, I had a figure that leaned more toward sumo wrestling. Oh, yeah, I could have been a gospel singer, because it seemed like no one cared about your size in that genre. But though I loved the Lord and had mad respect for the artists who brought glory to God that way, that's not what I wanted. I wanted to be on the other side of soul. My heart's desire was to be an R&B artist.

But the thing was, with singers like Beyoncé and Rhianna and Ciara leading the way, there just didn't seem to be room in R&B for a big girl like me.

Chapter 2

"Girl, I thought you were going to open up a can of whup-upside-the-head on old Miss Maggie!"

"Would you be quiet?" I couldn't believe how loud Devin was talking. He was supposed to be whispering, but the alcove of the church was small, and I was scared that everybody was going to hear him.

But even though I was trying to quiet Devin down, I had to work hard not to laugh. Not that I ever wanted to hurt old Miss Maggie, but "whup-upside-the-head"? That was some funny stuff.

"What are you young'uns over here laughing about?" In the small space, my father's voice was as strong as thunder. He sounded so serious, I wondered if he'd heard what Devin had said. I was almost scared to turn around and look at him. Even though I was twenty-two and living on my own (well, I was living in a dorm), my folks did not play. They didn't care how old I was; as long as they were paying the bills, they were in charge.

I held my breath and turned around. My parents were standing right there, shoulder-to-shoulder, smiling.

Whew! "We weren't laughing about anything," I rushed to say, 'cause I didn't want Devin explaining a thing. Over the years, he'd gotten us into enough trouble just by opening his mouth.

My father raised his left eyebrow like he always did when he didn't believe a word I said. "Well, it sure seems silly to me, standing around, laughing at nothing."

Chyanne came to the rescue. "You know how we are, Reverend Davenport."

I knew my father loved me and Skye, but there was no doubt that he loved Chyanne too. I guessed it was because her father died when she was just seven, in a really bad car accident. Chyanne had been in the car too, but she had been safe in the back seat when only the front of the car had been crushed.

I was only four when that happened, but I remembered some of it. And ever since then, Chyanne was the third Davenport sister. That meant with my parents she was treated the same way as me and Skye—with the good stuff and the bad.

Though, sometimes, it felt like Chyanne got a little more of the good stuff. Sometimes, my parents would cut Chyanne a little more slack, but that didn't bother me or Skye. The three of us just learned to use it to our advantage. That meant that whenever we wanted something, Chyanne was our spokesperson. Or when we were about to get in big trouble, we put Chyanne out in front.

Like now. All she had to say was that it was nothing, and my father just smiled and forgot all about it.

"So, what are you young people going to do for the rest of the day?" my mother asked.

My eyes got a little wide. I'd told her yesterday that we were going to have lunch with Skye; I couldn't figure out why she was bringing this up in front of my dad.

"Uh," I said, hoping Chyanne would pipe in with something. But just when I needed her the most, her mouth was closed tight. And, for once, so was Devin's. So I was on my own. With a breath I said, "We're meeting up with . . . Skye."

I spoke to my mother, but I looked at my dad. And the big old smile he'd just had was gone now. His eyes got small, he shifted his feet, and then he pressed his hands together in front of his face like he was about to pray.

"Well," he said, "give us a call when you get back to the dorm." He kissed my cheek and then walked away.

My mother looked at me with sad eyes, like she was sorry that she'd forgotten and had asked that question. She kissed me too. "Tell Skye that I love her and to call me."

My best friends and I watched my parents walk toward the back of the church, where I knew my father would pack up, then lock up the church. We stood there for a little while, and then Chyanne, Devin, and I looked at each other.

"Boy, this is some mess," Devin said.

Chyanne shook her head. "I know, I can't believe it's still going on."

"Neither can I. And it puts so much on me, being in the middle like this."

"We're in the middle with you, girl," Devin said all sadly. But in the next second, his eyes were bright and his smile was back and wide. "Being in the middle takes a lot of energy. So you heifers better come on so that I can get something to eat."

Chapter 3

My sister loved all the upscale places in the ATL and, today, Skye had chosen Shout for us to meet. Of course, by the time Chyanne, Devin, and I walked in, my always-on-time big sister was there.

"Hey!" She waved us over to a table for four. It was situated right in the center of the room, so that we could see everyone coming and going.

By the time I got over to Skye, I was grinning. Two weeks had passed since I'd last seen my sister. Over the last couple of weekends I'd had to do things with my parents. And anywhere my parents (or, should I just say, my dad) were, Skye wasn't.

"Girl, you look fresh!" I said, standing back after I hugged her. My sister, the fashionista, was wearing a strapless gray dress with a double bodice. The light wool fabric stopped right at her knees, and though the dress was sexy, it was conservative at the same time. Her black ankle-strapped four-inch heels made the whole thing *trés* chic.

That was Skye's style. She designed outfits that went from the office straight to the club. I couldn't figure out how she did that, but I guess that was the gift that God had given her.

"So, what's up, peeps?" she asked us after we all sat down.

"Girl, nothing but drama!" Devin breathed hard like he'd been through so much. He waved his hands in the air.

Skye frowned, and looked at me, then Chyanne, before she asked, "What kind of drama?"

"This is Devin's story," Chyanne said with her head buried in the menu. "Let him tell it, whatever it is."

"Hmph," was all Devin said.

Skye asked, "Would someone tell me what's going on?"

I looked at Devin. I was like Chyanne; I had no idea what drama he was talking about. His whole life was one big drama party. Who knew what kind of story he was going to tell us today? So I just motioned for him to take the floor, 'cause I wanted to hear about the drama too.

He grabbed his napkin from the glass, swung it in the air with a flourish, and then rested it on his lap. All of that and he hadn't said a word. See? Straight drama!

Finally, he said, "Well, your mother asked us where we were going and your father went off!"

"What?" Skye said. And Chyanne and I said the same thing. "My father didn't go off!"

"Yes, he did!" Devin insisted, snapping his fingers with each word. "After you told your mom that we were meeting Skye, your father went off," he said, waving his hand like he was shooing someone away. "He went off to the office or somewhere. . . ."

"Boy, please," Skye said.

Even though Skye laughed, I could tell she was relieved that Devin was just setting us all up and that our dad hadn't really gone off. But after we all stopped laughing, Skye asked me, "So, what did Daddy say when you told him you were meeting me?" She spoke, but her eyes were down like she was reading the menu, like she really didn't care.

I shrugged. "He didn't say anything, but Mama said to tell you that she loves you and to call her."

Skye shook her head. "I'd call her if she would just get her own phone. It's ridiculous in this day that someone doesn't have their own cell." She sighed. "But that's the only way, 'cause I'm not calling the house."

Chyanne put down her menu and stared at Skye like she was about to give her a lecture. Chyanne and Skye were the same age—they were three years older than me—but some-times, it felt like Chyanne was the oldest. She was always the mature, reasonable one. I always wondered if that had some-thing to do with losing her father. A lot of the old people in church said that she'd grown up before her time, watching her dad die like that.

Chyanne said, "You know this is going to have to end soon. Why don't you just go and talk to your father?"

"And say what?" Skye said. "He made it perfectly clear that if I didn't do things his way, if I didn't want to go into the min-istry, then I just needed to go out on my own. Well . . ." She left it right there, 'cause she didn't have to explain a thing. We all knew what had happened next.

We stayed quiet as the waiter came to our table and took our orders. And as I tried to decide between a salad and a hamburger, I thought about what Skye had said.

From the time I was little and realized that I had a big sis-ter, I had admired Skye. Not only because she was older, but she was fiercely independent. She just did what she wanted to do. If my parents said that we couldn't go over to a certain girl's house, and Skye wanted to, she found a way to make it happen. If we had a curfew and Skye missed it because she didn't want to leave the party, she just took her punishment. There were things that she'd done that my parents didn't even know about, and I would never tell. Like the nights she would put her stuffed animals under the covers, shape them like her body, and then sneak out of our bedroom window. She only did that a few times, and she was never gone for too long. But I was always scared . . . and just as impressed.

It wasn't like Skye was a bad kid. She wasn't hanging out with gangs or having sex, she was just being Skye. I used to think that a lot of it was because we were Reverend Daven-port's kids. And people put a lot on preacher's kids. But now, I wasn't so sure that was it. I think Skye was just being Skye.

From the time she was born, she just wanted to do things her way.

After the waiter walked away, Skye turned back to Chyanne. "So, here's the thing," she said, picking the conversation right backup. "I didn't start this war. My father did. He's the one who told me that if I thought I could do it on my own, then I should. And guess what, I did."

"Okay, so you won," Chyanne said, like it was no big deal. "Now, make peace and go home."

"Why? My dad let me go all the way to New York for three years, he let me go through FIT by myself, and he didn't lift a finger to help me. I had to struggle and fight, but I made it. All by myself."

"It wasn't totally by yourself," I jumped in. "Mama helped you all the time."

"Yeah, Mama, but not Daddy."

"Do you think your father didn't know that your mother was sending you money?" Chyanne asked. "Please, he knew every dollar. You know how he is. You were able to have that apartment in New York because of your mother *and* your father."

Skye shrugged, but I could tell she knew that Chyanne was right. Still, she wasn't about to admit it. The fact that Dad never supported her decision to attend the Fashion Institute of Technology made Skye ignore that he still made sure she had what she needed. There was no one more stubborn than Skye, except for my father. So with the two of them on opposite sides of this fight, the war was never going to end.

"Can we change the subject?" Devin whined. "All of this drama is making me lose my appetite. And you know, I've got to eat or else I'll lose my figure."

"You're the one who brought it up." Skye laughed.

Chyanne and Devin laughed, too, but I didn't. I chuckled, 'cause I didn't want them to think that anything was wrong, but I never laughed when people made jokes about their bodies. Because that just made me look at mine, and I didn't want to spend too much time doing that.

As we chatted, I glanced at Skye. With her smoky eyes, pouty lips, and perfectly applied makeup, she was the beauty of the family. Always had been. People said that we looked alike, but I couldn't see it. Maybe it was because she was so much smaller than me. I was three times the size of her size-six frame.

But that was not the only way we were different. Skye was determined to live her dream and become a fashion designer. Even if that meant doing it on her own, even if that meant losing her family, she was going to be who she wanted to be. And for that I so admired her. But if I told the whole truth, while I admired her, I was mad about it, too. Because that left a lot of pressure on me at home to make my parents, especially my dad, happy.

"So, sis, what's up with you?"

I shrugged. "Nothing. Just school. Glad to be graduating, I can tell you that."

"And after graduation, you're really going to work for that accounting firm?"

I nodded. "Yeah. That's what Dad . . ." I stopped, but everyone knew what I was going to say.

Skye shook her head. "I just can't believe it. So you're not going to give your singing a try at all? You're just going to let your dream die?"

The great thing about having people in my life like Skye, Chyanne, and Devin was that I could share all of my thoughts and dreams with them. And the bad thing about having them in my life was that I had shared all of my thoughts and dreams with them. For the last couple of years, the three of them had been after me to do something about what I wanted. But what was I supposed to do?

"Tell it," Devin said, holding up his hand like he was about to testify. "We've been trying to tell the girl that she needs to do something with that voice she has. Try out for *American Idol* or something."

"I don't know about *American Idol*," Skye said, "but you should do something. I mean, girl, we're in Atlanta. Do you know how many record producers are here?"

"Not to mention that we're young." Now, it was Chyanne putting in her two cents. "This is when we should go after our dreams."

I liked it better when we were all ganging up on Skye. I didn't want my friends looking at me. Because, if they looked too hard, they might see the real reason. But I hid behind the same old excuse.

"Daddy would never let me go out and sing all of that secular music."

I knew what Skye would do when I said that, and she did it. She just waved her hand, like my words and our dad didn't matter.

But Chyanne surprised me when she said, "You can't live your life for your father."

Skye and I both raised our eyebrows.

Chyanne continued, "What I'm saying is that you have to do you, but in a respectful way."

Skye rolled her eyes.

"I agree with Chy," Devin said. "Didn't you hear your father this morning?"

Skye asked, "What did he say?"

"Girlfriend, Daddy preached!" Devin sang. "He talked about how God knew us before we even came to earth and so He had plans and dreams that He wants us to achieve."

"And I think," Chyanne said, "that God is the one who puts certain desires in our hearts. So, if He wants it for us, He'll make a way. And if He wants it for us, then your father shouldn't have anything to say."

"Preach, counselor!" Devin said, and we all laughed again.

I agreed that was a good argument. One day, Chyanne was going to make a great lawyer. That was her dream.

As the waiter came back with our food, I looked at my friends. Talk about dreams and living them. Skye was an intern with Anne Barge, who got her start working under the head designer of Priscilla of Boston. Chyanne was in her third year of law school at Georgia State. She already had six-figure offers for three major law firms in New York. And Devin—he was a drama queen—still not sure of what he wanted to do, though he was really into hair styling and fashion. But I had no doubt that once he decided, no amount of drama would ever stop him from going after what he wanted.

Then there was me.

"Here you go," the waiter said, dropping in front of me the plate with the huge hamburger and stacked of fries. I glanced across the table. Devin and I had ordered the same thing, but Skye and Chyanne had both opted for salads.

For a moment, I pushed my hamburger aside. Maybe if I started today, if I ate a salad right now, this could be the beginning of me making some changes. And if I changed, maybe I would get the same kind of guts that Skye had. And if I got some guts, who knew what could I do?

But then I took a bite of my burger. And it tasted so good. I decided right then that I would make some changes. I would start with my weight.

But I would start tomorrow.

Chapter 4

I couldn't believe the number of boxes that we had stacked inside this truck.

"I told you, Jaylen; we should've gotten a dolly," Miles said as he hoisted a carton onto his shoulder.

All I did was grab the last box; I wasn't about to admit to my frat brother that he was right, even though he straight-up was. This job would have been quicker and easier on the back if I had sprung for something to help us. But when I rented this truck back in Berkeley on Wednesday, all I could think about was saving as much money as possible. This 2,500-mile trip was already putting a hurting on my empty wallet.

"So, what's up for tonight?" Quintin purred into his cell phone as Miles and I struggled up the two steps that led to the porch. Then, with one hand, Miles held the screen door open while I kicked in the front door. As I struggled inside, I glanced back. There was Quintin, just as he'd been since we arrived, leaning against the banister with his cell phone looking like it was growing out of his ear. Quintin hadn't helped us lift one box, or carried one computer from the truck. My boy was acting like he didn't have a single thing in these boxes, though straight up truth, probably half of this stuff was his. So now, not only had Miles and I driven Quintin's belongings across the country while he had relaxed in the friendly skies, but now he had us hauling his stuff inside like he was the king and we were his servant.

What I really wanted to do was leave Quintin's stuff right

in the truck, but there were two problems with that. One, we hadn't done the best job marking the boxes, so we had to open them to find out what was inside. And two, the truck was due to the Atlanta U-Haul office in just a couple of hours, and it was in my name. So I needed to get that sucker back before the hourly overage charges kicked in.

Inside the house, I dropped my box onto one of the dozens of others stacked high in the living room, then fell onto the sofa that was still covered with a sheet. Miles dropped down onto the other end, both of us still huffing and puffing like we were ready to blow this house down. But even though I was exhausted and pissed at Quintin for not helping, I wasn't all that mad. These were the first hours of my new life in the ATL. And as I glanced around at the stone fireplace in the living room and the chandeliers, I realized that this wasn't a bad way to start.

Leaning back, I closed my eyes. Hearing Miles breathing next to me, I knew he had done the same thing. I didn't have to look at him to know that he was as exhausted as I was. Our cross-country journey had begun before the sun had risen on Thursday. Miles and I, with that twenty-six-foot truck, tried to turn the thirty-six, hour trip into something closer to twenty-four. We made it through three states—California, Arizona, and New Mexico—before complete fatigue had set in. I had to talk Miles into that no-name motel off Interstate 40 because it wasn't like we knew anyone in Amarillo, Texas. Our plan had been to sleep for two hours, but six hours passed before we opened our eyes and hit the road again. The next part of the trip we planned better. We drove in two-hour shifts through Oklahoma, Arkansas, and Tennessee. Whoever wasn't driving was sleeping. Still, with just one more rest stop in Alabama, it had taken us forty-eight hours.

But we were here—my Kappa brothers, Quintin and Miles, and I—ready to make our presence known in the music industry.

The sound of the front door slamming made me sit up straight. Miles did the same.

"So, what's up?" Quintin asked, standing under the arch that separated the entryway from the living room. "Y'all taking a rest break?"

If Quintin weren't my frat brother, I would've hit him upside his head the way my mother used to do me when I was a kid and said something stupid.

"Yeah, we're resting all right," I said. "From driving across the country and then unloading that entire truck by ourselves."

Quintin's eyes got wide, like he couldn't believe what I was saying. "Y'all finished?"

"As if you didn't know," Miles said in his quiet manner.

"Ah, man, sorry 'bout that," Quintin said. Then, with two steps, he jumped over a couple of boxes and plopped down in one of the chairs across from us. "But y'all won't be mad at me for long." He grinned, as if his dimpled smile and charm would work on us the same way it did the ladies. "I hooked up a couple of things for us to do tonight. I wanted us to do it up right your first night in the ATL."

The way he said it, I guess he thought Miles and I were supposed to stand up and applaud. But if I had the energy to stand up, I wouldn't have been clapping.

I didn't say a word, but Miles said what I was thinking. "I ain't going nowhere but to bed after the last two days."

"Bed?" Quintin frowned at first, but two seconds later, he was grinning again. "Oh, you got some honey lined up here in Atlanta that you didn't tell us about." He reached over like he wanted to bump fists with Miles. "My man!" he said.

But Miles ignored him and so did I.

"What's up with y'all?" he asked, serious now.

"Miles just told you. We're tired."

"From just that little bit of driving?" He sucked his teeth.

"Man, we're young, and this is your first night in Atlanta. I've been scoping, trying to find all the happenings, and y'all just gonna flake out on me? What's up with that? You can't handle a little driving?"

He was asking us what was up, but I was just about to ask him the same thing—about all that "y'all" stuff. What was Quintin now, Southern gentleman? But I forgot about his newfound southern drawl the moment he started talking about what we couldn't handle.

"You try driving like a maniac across the country and see how you feel," I challenged Quintin.

"I would've felt just fine. If I'd known that you were going to bring all this drama, I would've driven with y'all."

My boy was straight-up lying! Quintin didn't believe in anything that was considered hard work, and driving all those miles and then lifting boxes was definitely hard work and against my man's religion.

But before I could call him the liar that he was, my cell vibrated on my hip. Peeping at the screen, I answered with a smile on my face.

"Uncle Matt, what's up?"

"Just checking on you," my uncle said. "Did you make it here yet?"

"Yeah, just a couple of hours ago. I was gonna call you later," I said, feeling a bit guilty. My mother's brother had been so excited about me coming to Atlanta, from the moment my mother called him to tell him that I was breaking her heart. I knew my mom and pops expected me to come right home to Los Angeles once I graduated from Berkeley, but by the time I finished my freshman year and had hooked up with Miles and Quintin, I knew I wasn't going back to L.A. Although many of the big record companies were still there, a lot of independent labels were rising up in places like Minneapolis and Atlanta. During our sophomore year, when we decided that we were going to be the next hot thing, we'd decided that there was no need to compete for talent and time with the big boys.

"We need to move to Hot-lanta," Quintin had said.

And Miles and I agreed.

I'd waited until my senior year to tell my folks. And from the way my mother cried, you would have thought I'd stabbed her straight in the heart. And that's just what she told everyone.

"You try to raise your children right and what do they do to you? They grow up and move to Atlanta!"

But once my moms realized that I wasn't going to change my mind, she got over it and started calling folks to see who she could get to look out for me. As if I needed someone to take care of me. My moms didn't get it; I was a grown man now. A broke man, but grown nonetheless.

"Well, I'm glad you made it safely." My uncle's voice pulled me back into the conversation.

"Yeah, Miles and I are 'bout to take the truck over to U-Haul, and then we're gonna just chill from that long ride."

"I understand. I was hoping, though, that tomorrow you could come to church with me."

I closed my eyes and rubbed my forehead. It's not that I had anything against church. I was raised to love the Lord. But straight-up truth, I hadn't been attending regular services in college. In fact, I could count on one hand the number of times I'd been to church, and still have a couple of fingers left over.

"And then," my uncle continued saying, "you can come by the house and have dinner with your Aunt Lily and me."

"Ah . . . Uncle Matt . . ."

It must've been the way I stuttered that made him add, "This is not just about wanting you to go to church. Our executive board is looking for a minister of music to lead our choir. We want a fresh voice and I already told them about you. You haven't found another job yet, have you?"

As soon as my uncle said, "job," I sat up straight. No, I didn't have a job, and didn't have many prospects. Both Quintin and Miles had been hooked up, but with their degrees in business and IT, respectively, they'd been able to find employment, even during these tough times. But with my music degree, and wanting to stay in the industry, it had been rough going for me. So this announcement by my uncle was coming at the best of times.

"Hell, yeah." And then, I remembered who I was talking to. "I mean, yes, sir, I'm interested."

My uncle was quiet for a moment. I guess he was wondering if he'd made a mistake by recommending his foul-mouthed nephew for a position as a minster of anything. But my uncle was cool and he knew I wasn't really like that.

"Okay, well, I just thought it might be a good idea for you to come, get a feel of our church and Reverend Davenport. We're gonna be talking to several others, but you can come by and meet with the board on Tuesday."

"Really, that soon?" By now, I could see both Quintin and Miles sitting up, listening in. I knew my boys couldn't wait for me to get off to hear my news. Anything that was good for one of us would be good for all of us, since we were in this together. "I will definitely be there." I started to ask my uncle about the pay, but then I thought, what did it matter? Anything they were offering was more than I was making now. "Okay, I'll see you tomorrow," I said right after my uncle gave me all the details for the church. Clicking off my phone, I leaned back, not feeling so tired after all.

"What's up?" Quintin asked.

"Looks like I have a lead on a job."

"That's great," Miles said.

Quintin wanted the details. But when I told him about my conversation, he frowned.

"Why you gonna mess with that?" he asked.

It was my turn to frown, because I thought my reason was obvious. "I need a job."

"Man, you don't need no job like that. What's church gonna do for you when we're trying to build Tru Harmony?"

"Ah . . . it's gonna help me pay my way."

"I told you, we got you," Quintin said.

Yeah, that's what my boys had said. That since we were living rent free in one of Miles's parents' homes, they would cover me for anything else so that I could be the one to focus on geting our company going. But I wasn't like that. There was no way I was going to sit around all day while Quintin and Miles worked. I was gonna be a man about it, and if I could find a job, then I could work.

"You don't need to be messing with those Bible thumpers." Quintin kept on talking like he always did.

"Look," I said in a tone that was meant to let Quintin know that we were not going to talk about this anymore. "It's just a lead, not a definite. But after the interview, if it's something I think I can work, and they like me, it's on. I'm going for it."

"Man!" Quintin said, jumping up. "So how we gonna get our label started if you working all day at some church?" He didn't even give me a chance to answer him. Just stomped out of the room like he was some kid.

Miles sat back; he was so used to me and Quintin going at it. At least this time he didn't have to jump into the middle.

"So, what do you think?" I asked Miles. Not that what he said was going to change my mind.

He shrugged. "Do you. I don't see how working could hurt; you might even get some divine inspiration."

"That's what I was thinking. You don't have to worry; nothing's gonna stop me from focusing on Tru Harmony. Trust that."

"I know. I know you can handle it. All three of us can."

I nodded, and leaned right back on the couch. I needed to

get my butt up and take that truck down to U-Haul. But I just wanted a moment. To think about being in Atlanta, and how, with my uncle's call, everything was coming together.

I didn't have the job yet. And, as my uncle had said, they were interviewing quite a few people. But I had a secret weapon: a praying mama. I knew that when I called her later about this, she'd get right on her knees. Then, it would be a wrap.

I had a good feeling about this. I was on my way. Or really, I should say, we were on our way. *The world had better get ready for me, Miles, Quintin, and Tru Harmony.*

Chapter 5

It was more than just this stiff-collared white shirt I had on that was choking me. It was the air, too, which was thick with tension.

As I sat at the head of the long table with six people sitting on one side, and six on the other, I had a feeling that my uncle didn't have a clue. He said that these people wanted to see me. Man, he didn't know what he was talking about. Not with the way the people on the left side of the room stared me down as if they wanted me to get up and get out of their precious church.

But, then, there were the people on the right side, mostly ladies, and my uncle, who just smiled and nodded at every word I said.

"So, young man, you've never had any kind of experience working inside a church?"

I looked straight ahead at the man who was sitting at the other end of the board table: Reverend Davenport. I'd answered a ton of questions already about my experience, but his question was the first thing he'd said since I'd walked into this conference room thirty minutes ago.

Funny, the reverend had been all laughter, full of energy and everything when he preached on Sunday. I'd actually enjoyed the sermon about Queen Vashti and Queen Esther. The way the reverend broke it down made the story something that I could relate to. But today, there was no sign of the man who had stood in the pulpit on Sunday. The man sitting all the way at the other end of this conference table wore a frown so deep, it looked like he had crevices in his forehead.

"No, sir," I said, finally answering Reverend Davenport's question. "I've never worked in a church, even though, as I said, I am a Christian. But what I believe is that music is music and—"

The reverend raised his hand, stopping me. He glared at me so hard, it made the collar of my shirt feel even tighter. "Music is *not* music, son," he said in a tone that let me know he thought I had some lessons to learn, and that he was going to be the one to school me. "There is nothing that can compare to the music that is set aside for the Lord. And the people who sing that other music . . ."

He waved his hand in the air as if anyone who sang anything besides gospel was only doing the devil's work. Well, since I'd just told these people that my ultimate goal was to start my own R&B label, I guess this was the end of this road.

Reverend Davenport looked at me as if he was waiting for me to speak, but I didn't know what to say. Not that I really thought he cared about what I might say. All I wanted to do at this point was get up and get out.

But just when I was about to rise, one of the women—a younger one—from the right side of the table said, "Well, young man, you have been the most impressive one we've met with so far."

That was a shocker!

Slowly, I edged right back into my seat, wanting to hear more of what the blond lady had to say.

"What I like about you," she began, and then looked around the table, "and I'm not trying to speak for anyone else, is that you have dreams you're passionate about. And that passion will always come out in music."

"Yes." The women and my uncle who were sitting near her nodded and smiled.

I didn't have to look at the other side of the table to know that the opposite was going on.

"Well," my uncle said, standing up, "if no one has any more questions . . ."

Now, the whole table was in accord; they shook their heads as if they all couldn't wait to get rid of me.

Uncle Matt nodded at me. I guessed that was my signal to stand up and get out. So I did. But before I turned to the door, I said, "Thank you all so much for your consideration. When I came to church on Sunday with Uncle Matt, I knew this was a different kind of place. A church that related to the people, and didn't just preach messages that went over our heads." I looked right into Reverend Davenport's eyes when I said, "I could feel the anointing here, and would love to be a part of this ministerial team."

Well, the little prep talk that Miles had given me worked because even the reverend nodded. He still didn't smile, but at least his frown wasn't so deep.

Slowly, I stepped to the door where my uncle shook my hand and patted me on the back. "We'll be in touch," he whispered.

As soon as I stepped into that hallway and my uncle closed the door behind me, I broke into a trot. I couldn't get away fast enough; I had walked in with such hope, but, now, it didn't look so good. It was too bad, too, because the hours would have been perfect: meeting with the choir for rehearsals twice a week on Tuesdays and Thursdays, and then Sunday services. I certainly could've handled that. And Quintin would've been happy. No way could he have complained about my time being taken away from Tru Harmony.

By the time I got to the front of the church, my tie was off and I had unfastened the top two buttons on my shirt. My mind was already on other things, like the fact that I did have to find a job since it didn't look like this one was going to come through.

I was deep inside my head when I heard all this laughter. In front of me, there were three kids, well, not kids really. They looked younger than me, probably college students, who were leaning on a Ford truck that was parked right next to me.

I slowed my roll so that I could check out the group: two girls, one guy, though even from feet away, I could tell that the guy was gay. I hated to put labels on anyone, but it was the way the dude was dressed—better than the two girls and his hair was done up, too.

I checked out the females. One looked like she should've been in somebody's video, or maybe a movie, she was that fine. The other one was cute too—a big girl, who seemed to have her own style.

As I got closer, they stopped talking.

The guy nodded. "Whassup?" he said in a voice that was deeper than I'd expected.

I nodded back, but it was hard to take my eyes away from the girls. Finally, I hit the remote to the BMW and slipped into Miles's car. I tried to focus on just putting the key in the ignition and going about my business. But I couldn't help it; I wanted one last look. And when I turned to glance out the window, I was shocked when she was looking straight at me. Through the window, I could see her light brown eyes filled with clarity and laughter. She looked at me as if she knew me, as if she could see through me.

I was mesmerized. But only for a second.

I hit the accelerator and the tires screeched against the gravel, leaving a trail of gray dust behind me. Now, I was really sorry that I wasn't going to be working at Greater Faith. Because if Reverend Davenport was drawing in the honeys like that, this was where I wanted to be.

"Dang!" I whispered to myself as soon as I had that thought. How could I be thinking about church girls like that? I felt like I needed to pull over to the side of the road and repent, but since I was in the middle of traffic and about to roll onto Interstate 20, I couldn't. So, I just asked God to forgive me for being such a heathen. "I'm just a man, made of flesh," I said, repeating what I'd heard some of the men in my family say. But then, I added my own spin. "But dang, Lord, why'd you have to make the honeys so fine?"

I laughed a little, then got real serious. It was time to get back to business. Time to think about how I was gonna find a job.

Chapter 6

This was almost as bad as hell week. Well, maybe not—nothing was as tough as crossing and becoming a proud member of Kappa Alpha Psi Fraternity, Inc. No, this was more like finals, when every hour was devoted to studying. Yeah, that's kind of the way the last week had felt. Not that it was bad, naw, this was all good. It was just *a lot* of good stuff.

It started a week ago, last Tuesday. When I walked out of that church, my mind had been on nothing except finding a job; that is, if you didn't count the few minutes I spent checking out that female who'd been standing in the parking lot. But once I jumped inside Miles's car, my mind left the honey and turned right back to the money, which I did not have. Quintin and Miles kept telling me not to worry about it, but I wasn't trying to hear that. A grown man had to take care of his, and that's just what I was going to do.

That had been my thought as I parked Miles's car in front of the three-bedroom house that was one of the many properties that Miles's parents owned all over the country. But I didn't have any time to wallow in the elegant surroundings that were really too high class for three frat brothers just out of college. My phone vibrated on my hip the moment I put the key in the door.

At first, when I saw Uncle Matt's number flash across the screen, I wanted to ignore it. I figured if he was calling me this soon, then I had definitely embarrassed him in front of his Christian friends. But for some reason, I picked up anyway.

"Congratulations, young man," he said right after I said hello. "If you want it, you've got it. The board of directors of Greater Faith Baptist wants to offer you the position of assistant minister of music."

"That quick?" I asked, instead of saying thank you. I couldn't believe they'd gotten back to me so fast. Then, my uncle explained what they'd already told me, that they didn't want to waste any time and were ready to move forward.

"And," my uncle added, "you impressed so many on the board that they didn't see why we should keep on interviewing when we'd found the one we wanted. It's not like they had to check you out. I'm the best reference you could have."

I really wanted to make it on my own, but at that moment, I was so grateful for the hookup. I thanked my uncle, before he asked me to turn around and come right back to Greater Faith. From that moment, I was stone busy, running back and forth to the church, sometimes two and three times a day, meeting with individual board members, trying to get their vision. Everyone was cordial enough; even the ones who didn't seem to want me at first seemed to be cool once I'd been selected. Even Brother Steve had me sitting in his office as he laughed and joked as if we were old buddies. At first, I wasn't feeling that, but then he told me he was frat, and that changed everything.

The only dark side in the last week had been my meeting with Reverend Davenport. The reverend was the single person who didn't seem to be too happy with my selection. It made me wonder how I'd been chosen if the man in charge didn't want me. I hoped that I wasn't caught up in some church politics; though, as soon as I met with the reverend, I stopped thinking that. It didn't feel like politics at all; it felt personal.

During our meeting, Reverend Davenport said, "There were quite a few on the board who found your ability and knowledge for music impressive," as if he wasn't one of the impressed people. "I just hope that you will make Greater Faith your priority."

"Yes, sir, I will," I'd told him. But my words didn't change the scowl on his face.

"I know you want to go out there in the world and make it big time with all of that secular music." Reverend Davenport had said "secular" as if it were a curse word.

"I will never let what I do outside of church get in the way of what's going on in here."

He shook his head, and looked at me as if I didn't know a thing. "What you do outside should be the same as what you do in here. It should all be for the Lord. Only the things that we do for Him will last. Only those things will count."

I nodded, because I wasn't about to get into any kind of argument with the reverend. But what I really wanted to tell him was that just because a song didn't tell the story of Jesus didn't mean that it wasn't worthy to be sung. But since I wanted—no, I needed this job—I kept my lips smacked together like I agreed with every word the reverend said.

Then, once I made it past the reverend, I sat down with Ms. Carolyn, the church secretary. She had me sign a ton of papers before she loaded me down with everything about Greater Faith Baptist: the church doctrine, the bylaws, et cetera, et cetera, et cetera.

I made it through all of those days, and now I was standing next to the keyboard in front of the choir. My parents had raised me right, so I never spent a lot of time talking about anybody, but this choir was surely a motley crew. I mean, most churches had the choirs separated by groups. But, at Greater Faith, the youth sat right next to the seniors. From the young guy with pink-tipped spiked hair to an older lady with hair that was so blond, I needed to put on my sunglasses to stop the glare. It didn't matter though; I was gonna rock whatever they gave me to work with.

"So, I just want to say once again that it really is an honor for me to be standing here before you," I said after I'd introduced myself and given them a short verbal résumé.

I knew the choir had been prepared for my being here tonight; Brother Steve told me so. But there were only a few smiles on the faces of the thirty-seven people who sat in front of me. Most wore curious expressions, like I was a stranger from another land. But then there were some who, like the folks in the board meeting, sat with their arms folded, and scowls on their faces as if they'd been training with Reverend Davenport. Although I hadn't quite won over Reverend Davenport, I was sure that I would get the choir on my side. After all, I had charm. And I could sing. Singing always impressed a singer.

"I want you to know that I'm not coming in to make major changes. I was here last Sunday and I heard y'all rock, so I know what you can do."

When I said that, some of the scowls disappeared. As I said, I had charm.

"I want to shake up the songs, not the singers."

There were a few more smiles, but still nothing but the deepest of frowns from the blond woman who sat front and center. Her arms were still crossed as if she planned to never let me in.

"But I do plan to bring a taste of Jaylen Richards to our sound. I want us to be different, not another Kirk Franklin-sounding choir."

Now, everyone nodded in agreement. Everyone except the blond woman.

"I don't want to keep you later than usual, so let's get started." I reached into my bag for the sheet music to the song I'd written. Sitting down at the keyboard, I said, "Tell me what you think of this."

Then, I hit the first bars and began to sing, "Though I walk through the valley of the shadows, I didn't know how I would make it out. Had troubles in my life, and it seemed like me no one cared about."

I'd started this song the night my uncle told me that I had the job. It had taken me days to make it tight; usually, I could write the basic part of a song in a couple of hours. But for this gig, I wanted to come out my first Sunday fresh!

Leaning back, I closed my eyes, and my fingers danced across the keyboard. I sang the way I'd been singing my whole life. I played the keyboard with so much passion. Though I'd had extensive training growing up and at Berkeley, this still came so naturally to me. Music was part of my soul.

I sang, never opening my eyes, just looking at the light behind my lids. There was not a word I sang nor a note I played that wasn't a part of me. At the end, I waited a couple of seconds before I slowly opened my eyes. The members of the choir were staring at me once again. But this time not like I was a foreigner, but as if I were from another planet totally. Then, they did something I didn't expect. They clapped.

"We're gonna sing that?" one of them yelled out.

I grinned and nodded. "Yeah, we're gonna sing that on Sunday, so we better get started. First," I said as I glanced around the choir stand, "we're gonna need a soloist."

Before I could finish my words, the blond lady raised her hand.

"I'm the soloist," she said, like she was the one making the decision.

I could feel my eyebrows coming together in a frown, so I smiled to change the expression on my face. "Okay, what's your name?" I asked, holding out my hand to shake hers.

"Sister Maggie," she told me.

Behind her, I heard some of the younger ones in the back row giggle.

"Okay, Sister Maggie, come on up here."

For the first time since she'd walked into the room, she smiled. My eyes glanced through the whole choir stand, and that was when I noticed her—the girl from the parking lot. I hadn't recognized her before, because today she wore a Spelman hat. But it was her for sure. I knew because I could see her eyes. Just like last week, her eyes smiled at me before her lips did.

I shook my head a little so that I would stop staring at her. "Anyone else?"

"Anyone else what?" Sister Maggie asked.

"Is there anyone else who wants to try out for the solo?"

"Try out?" Sister Maggie looked at me as if I'd lost my mind. "I told you," she added, her voice a bit stronger now, "I'm the soloist."

I didn't even try to hide my frown this time. "How do you know? This song might not be right for you."

"Every song is right for me," she said, twisting her neck as if she were straight from the hood and thirty years younger. "I'm the soloist, have always been the soloist, and will always be the soloist." She pressed her lips together as if she was trying to hold back what she really wanted to say.

Now, as I said, charm had always worked for me. But I wasn't feeling charming right now. What I wanted to do was to tell this old lady to sit down. But, as I also said, my parents had raised me right.

So I took a deep breath, and remembered that I was James and Pamela's son. "Sister Maggie, I'm really glad to know that you've been the soloist; that means that you can really sing."

She nodded and stuck her chest back out as if she'd shown me something.

"But I'm sure that there are other people in the choir who can really sing too."

Sister Maggie looked like she wanted to slap me.

I kept right on explaining. "And the thing is, not every solo is perfect for everyone. I want to find the best voice for this song. Does that make sense?"

Now, she looked as if she wanted to slap me twice. But she had enough sense to step back, knowing that if she didn't, she'd look like a fool.

"Make sense?" I repeated, purposely putting her on the spot.

"I guess," she growled. But one thing was for sure, Sister Maggie hadn't lost her confidence, because she added, "Bring 'em on!" as if she was ready to give someone a beat-down. "Try us all out," she said, waving her hands at her choir partners. I didn't miss the way she stared down everyone behind her, as if she dared anyone to even think about stepping up.

She may have intimidated them, but not me. I didn't care what she had to say.

"Okay, who else wants to try out?" I asked.

When no one raised their hand, I let my eyes wander. But people looked down, looked up, looked away; everyone had stopped looking at me. I glanced at the back row, and paused when my eyes once again settled on the girl. Her arms were straight by her side, and though I couldn't tell for sure, it looked like she was sitting on her hands. Now, she could have been doing that because her hands were cold. But I doubted it, because even though it was March outside, it felt like August inside the sanctuary. So, if she wasn't cold, there was only one other reason she was sitting on her hands: she was trying to stop herself from volunteering for the solo.

"Why don't you come up here?" I said, looking straight at her.

Her eyes widened just a little bit, but she didn't move. Just stared at me as if I couldn't possibly be talking to her.

"You." I pointed, just to be clear.

My direct acknowledgment didn't make a difference. The girl didn't move until the guy with the spiked hair sitting next to her nudged her a bit.

She shook her head slightly, as if she wanted me to change my mind, but I wasn't going to. I was just about to walk to the back and pull her up when she finally stood. She moved so slowly, like she was trying to let the whole hour go by so that she wouldn't have to sing.

For a second, I wondered why she was so hesitant. Could she have a voice like a bear? Well, I was soon going to find out.

When she finally stood in front of me, I handed the sheet music to both Sister Maggie and the girl. "Either of you have any questions?"

They shook their heads.

I asked, "Who wants to go first?"

Sister Maggie pointed at the girl. "Let Simone go."

Simone. Her name sounded like a song, and right then I knew that I didn't have to worry about whether she could sing. Before Simone opened her mouth, it was the instinct inside of me that let me know she could blow. Now, I couldn't wait.

"Okay, Simone," I said, taking my place behind the keyboard. I played the first few bars, then looked up at her. She was shaking, as if she was nervous. But then she opened her mouth. And released exquisiteness.

"Now I know that I can make it through by and by. Because all things are possible with God on my side," she sang.

It took everything I had to keep playing, because all I wanted to do was sit back and listen to babygirl sing.

"You brought me through it all, Lord." Her voice filled the sanctuary. Her range was wide, and, truthfully, this song didn't do this young lady any kind of justice. I wanted to stop playing, run home right now, and write something special for Simone.

Finally, she finished. For a moment, everyone stared . . . until they started applauding. And stomping. Like they'd just seen a concert or something. I was supposed to be impartial, but, dang, even I had to stand up and clap.

I wondered if Sister Maggie could get close to that. But it looked like I wasn't gonna find out. Because while we were cheering for Simone, Sister Maggie rolled her eyes and slinked back to her seat. I guess she wasn't about to go up against that.

I said, "That was incredible, Simone." Turning back to the rest of the choir, I said, "But I still want everyone to try out who wants to."

While everyone else shook their heads, Sister Maggie crossed her arms and rolled her eyes at me and Simone.

"Okay." I shrugged, and turned back to the young lady who had just mesmerized all of us. "Well, Simone, it looks like you'll be singing the solo on Sunday."

"Really?" She looked as thrilled as I felt, and she must've been, because before she or I could think about it, she threw her arms around me and hugged me as if I'd just given her a gift.

Simone felt so good that all I could do was hug her back. But, suddenly, her arms fell from my neck, and she took two quick steps back away from me. I frowned, not sure what had happened. Her glance was in my direction, but beyond me. I turned around so that I could see what had taken her attention away. And I looked into the eyes of Reverend Davenport.

His face was tight with the same scowl that he wore the day we met, and I began to wonder if he'd reserved that disdainful smirk just for me. When he shook his head slightly, I frowned.

Quickly, I turned and faced Simone, but she had gone back to her last-row seat in the choir stand. And, once again, she looked like she was sitting on her hands.

I had no idea what that was about; it seemed as if the reverend was upset about something. He should've come into the sanctuary a little earlier. Maybe if he'd heard Simone singing, he would have been in a better mood. Well, whatever, I figured. He'd be straight on Sunday, because with the way Simone could sing, she and I were going to turn Greater Faith Baptist Church out!

Chapter 7

This was how fame felt. I was sure about that.

I stood in front of the choir, exactly the way Miss Maggie had been doing for as long as I could remember. And I stayed there as the sanctuary exploded with applause and cheers. It felt like they'd been clapping for five minutes. And all of the applause was for me!

I grinned so hard my cheeks hurt. But my face didn't ache just from being happy today; I'd been grinning like this for the last week. My smiley face had started when Minister Jaylen picked me to be the soloist. At that moment, I felt as if I were living inside someone else's dream, though at first, it wasn't all good.

I'd had no plans to stand up and fight Miss Maggie for the solo. I was just like everybody else; I was just going to let her have it. As Miss Maggie said, it'd always been that way. But Minister Jaylen forced me to get up. And once he put that music into my hands, I wasn't going to half step; I was gonna bring it for real. When the choir cheered and Miss Maggie sat down, I knew I'd done good. I was so happy that I hugged Minister Jaylen, shocking him—and myself—in the process.

That was when my dad walked into the sanctuary. Boy, if looks could kill, Minister Jaylen and I would both be laid up in some cemetery right about now. I wasn't sure what my father was upset about. It could have been because I was all up on the new minister, or that I had been given the solo. I never found out what the deal was, because all my father did was turn and walk right out of the sanctuary without saying a word. Even later that night, when he called to make sure that I'd arrived at my dorm safely, he didn't mention anything about what had gone down at church. I guessed he didn't want to talk about it . . . and that worked for me, because it wasn't like I wanted to explain a thing to him.

But aside from worrying about my father, the last week had been wonderful. Jaylen may have been young (I found out that he was just a year older than me), but he worked us way more than Brother Steve ever did. And he made me work the hardest, though I didn't complain. There were nights after rehersal when Jaylen and I practiced alone in the choir room, working through every detail of the song. What was best was that Minister Jaylen even allowed me to change the words of one verse. He told me he respected my opinion. He treated me like a real singer, the same way everybody in the church was treating me right now.

I glanced into the sanctuary, and Chyanne and Devin were on their feet like everyone else, cheering me on. Right in front of them, in the first pew, was my mother, standing too, clapping and smiling. It was my mom who made me think about my dad. I glanced to my right and saw him. He was the only person in the whole church who was still sitting, there in his great big ol' chair in the middle of the pulpit. When he saw me looking at him, he pushed himself up as if he didn't want to, but had to. But that was all he did, just stand. It was as if he couldn't find a way to bring his hands together. It was as if standing was the best he could do.

I felt a little pain in my heart, but I wasn't about to let my dad take away all my joy of these minutes.

Finally, I turned to the man who made this all possible, and he was cheering the loudest. It was Minister Jaylen's smile that made mine wider.

Yup, this had to be what fame felt like.

Finally, grudgingly, I moved my feet and went back to the last row. When I got to my seat, Minister Jaylen motioned for the whole choir to sit down. I did, but I didn't want to. I wanted to stand up and sing again so that I could feel that good feeling over and over and over.

But then my father slowly walked to the podium. He waited for a moment, for the people in the sanctuary to settle down. Then, he said, "Saints, turn in your Bibles to . . ."

I was so shocked that I didn't even hear what scripture my father wanted us to study. That was all he was going to say? I wanted to yell out for him to stop and acknowledge me and the choir the way he always did when Miss Maggie sang her solos. But even though I tried to stare him down, my father was already in preachin' mode, as if my song never happened.

The pain in my heart that I felt a moment ago was so much stronger now. Maybe it was just that my dad couldn't accept me as a singer because he couldn't see me as one. Maybe all he saw when he looked at me was a fat girl who would be better off being an accountant.

Why did I keep doing this to myself? When was I going to realize that I needed to stop all this dreaming and just do what was best?

I peeked over at Carlton to see what scriptures my father wanted us to read. And as I turned the pages of my Bible, I made a promise that I was never going to do this again. I was going to stop with the big dreams and just focus on reality. I needed to get excited about being a paper-pushin' accountant. I could be good at that; plus, top accountants made lots of money. I just needed to keep it real and keep it moving.

But what was I supposed to do with all of these feelings inside of me? I lifted my eyes from the Bible and peeked over at Minister Jaylen. This was all his fault. Because after working with Minister Jaylen, I had really started to believe.

Chapter 8

I didn't want to brag, but it was hard not to as I sat in the middle of Chili's. The Hawks were playing on every big screen in the place, and, though my boys were the Lakers, I still liked a good game of b-ball.

"So, what did you guys think?" I asked once the waitress dropped the hamburger platters in front of me, Quintin, and Miles.

"That's what's up," Miles said. He took a sip of his Budweiser, even though we hadn't been out of church for more than an hour.

I'd dragged Quintin and Miles out of bed early this morning and made them go to Greater Faith with me. Actually, it wasn't all that bad. This was my first Sunday, and even though Quintin, especially, tried to give me a hard time about having to get up so early after a long Saturday night, I knew my brothers were going to be there for me.

Miles had given me his opinion, and now I wanted to know what Quintin thought; so I asked him directly.

He took a sip of his beer as if he needed time to think. Then, he said, "Can't front. Y'all rocked it." He was still talking with his newfound Southern accent. But then, as quickly as he gave that compliment, he took it away. "I still think working at that church is bogus. You haven't done a thing to build our label."

"What are you talking about?" I asked with a frown. "I told you, since I've been at the church, I can't stop writing. Man, I've got an arsenal of songs ready for Tru Harmony."

I'd told Quintin and Miles earlier this week that the church had inspired me, though that wasn't the total truth. It wasn't the church alone; Simone was the one. Her voice got me going. Made me want to write song after song after song.

"Okay, so you've been writing," Quintin said. "But who are you writing for? Are we even close to discovering the next hottest thang?" he asked with a twang. "What about that? You can't have a label without talent."

"I'm working on it," I said as Simone's face flashed in my mind. Whenever I thought about who was going to be the first to be recorded on Tru Harmony, I saw Simone. With her voice and that incredible face, she'd be the perfect one.

But I wasn't about to say anything to Quintin or Miles, because I hadn't said anything to Simone. It surprised me, actually, that Simone hadn't said anything about wanting to be a singer. I couldn't figure that out. Back at Berkeley, girls with half of Simone's talent were always bumping up against Miles, Quintin, and me, trying to get us to agree to record them, even though we didn't even have a company. But the whole time I'd worked with Simone, she'd stayed focused on our one song as if she didn't have any dreams beyond the Greater Faith choir.

"We can't call ourselves a label if all we have is a name and a couple of songs." He took another swig of his beer. "Man, I'm not even trying to stay at Verizon," he said, sounding like he was already complaining about his new job, even though he'd only been there two weeks.

"It takes time," Miles said, always the rescuer. "And it—"

Quintin held up his hand. "I know, I know. It takes time and patience. I have both; just as long as we're moving."

"We're moving," I said.

Quintin nodded, and then held out his fist. Miles and I raised our hands and we bumped knuckles like we always did—our way of making a pact.

I sat back as we turned our attention to the basketball game. There were moans throughout the restaurant; the Celtics were walking all over the Hawks. But as Quintin and Miles talked smack with a couple of other patrons, my thoughts were on Simone and Tru Harmony. She had told me that she was a senior at Spelman, so she probably had all of her life plans together. But I had something for her, something that would change her life. It might take me a minute if all Simone had ever dreamed of was being a teacher or something. But I knew I could show her that she could have so much more. Yeah, I'd be able to get Simone on board; I was sure of that. And once I did, I had no doubt that Tru Harmony would take off.

Chapter 9

I set the last platter of macaroni and cheese in the center of the dining room table, then took my seat across from my mother. From the head of the table, my father reached out his hands, and my mother and I bowed our heads as we held on to my dad.

This was our tradition, Sunday dinner at the Davenports. No matter how many people were here (and usually it was just the three of us) my mom prepared a feast that most people only had at Thanksgiving. Our Sunday dinners were straight out of the soul food manual: fried catfish, fried chicken, green bean casserole, collard greens, rice and gravy, biscuits, and a whole lot more. It was all here.

"Amen!" my mother and I said with my father.

I unfolded the napkin that I'd just folded when I helped my mother set the table. Even though it was just the three of us tonight, the table was set formally, just the way my father liked it.

"So," my dad said as he scooped a heaping spoonful of yams onto his plate. "Have you heard any more from Ernst & Young?"

Forget about the preliminaries—it never took my father very long to get to the point. At least, this was what I thought the point of these dinners was: to make sure that I did exactly what he wanted me to do.

I shook my head as I plucked two biscuits from the basket, but then put back one. "There's not much for them to say," I told him. "I already accepted the offer, and, as soon as school's out, I'll go back into the internship program before I begin officially in September."

My father put his fork down and frowned. "Intern? So, you don't officially have the job?"

I nodded. "Yeah, I do. This last phase is more like an orientation so that I can get acclimated to the company. But I'm not assigned to a senior staffer or given any cases until September."

My father's beam was back. "Have I told you how proud we are of you?" he asked.

As I bit off a piece of chicken, I nodded. Yeah, my dad always told me he was proud of me . . . whenever he was talking about my boring corporate job. But with anything else, like my singing, his pride went right out the window.

"You've brought so much joy to our hearts," he said.

I glanced at my mother, and she was smiling. But it wasn't the way that she'd been smiling this morning after my solo. What she had on now was a polite smile. This morning, she was the one who was filled with pride.

So, why didn't she stand up for me? Why did she let my father control everything?

I didn't know why I was asking myself these questions when I knew the answers. My mother truly saw herself as an Old Testament helpmate. Her role was to stand behind my father, no matter what he said, no matter what he did. Even if she disagreed, she pretended to agree. It was ridiculous to me; how could a woman in 2010 be thinking this way?

"Hasn't she, Treece?" My father's voice brought me right back to the dinner table. "Hasn't Simone just made us proud?"

"Definitely!" My mother said the right word, right on cue.

I wanted to roll my eyes, but that was one thing about Theresa Davenport: she may have been a Stepford Wife, but she was also an old-school Black mother. And she would have snatched me and my eyes if I tried some stuff like that with her. So all I did was smile and nod a silent thank you.

"Yup," my father kept on. "I'm so proud." Then, his voice got lower and I knew what was coming. I could have almost said the words with him. "Yes, you've made us so proud. Not like your sister."

I didn't know how my father did that. Here he was, this big-time pastor, always preaching about God's forgiveness, but he wasn't willing to forgive his own daughter. Though really, there was nothing to forgive Skye for; she'd just moved on and done what she wanted to do with her life. And because of that, not only would our father not forgive her, but he bashed her every chance he got. Whatever happened to controlling the tongue?

But do you think I was going to ask my father any of those questions? Nope. Like my mom, he was old school too, though he would have said that he was just following scripture: spare the rod, spoil the child. Even though I was twenty-two, if I got too far out of line, the good reverend would have found a rod to make sure I remembered what was up.

Then came the killer words, "Skye has always been such a disappointment."

Those were the ones that got to me all the time. How could he say that about his own daughter?

But he always did, and that was why I was going to stick to my promise. Because no matter how mad my father made me, I knew for a fact that he loved me. And I loved him too. I didn't think I'd be able to breathe if he ever said he was disappointed in me.

So I took a deep breath and then exhaled all of my dreams. Really, what did my dreams matter when my father had given me so much? What did my dreams matter when I could make my father happy?

That's what I needed to do. Make my father happy, and find a way to make myself happy at the same time.

Chapter 10

I had figured out a way!

When Simone and I were practicing, she'd suggested a change to "Keep Moving" (another song I wrote), which was spot on. I'd asked her then if she was a songwriter and she'd just laughed. But I wasn't going to let her laugh it off today.

"We should write a song together," I said to Simone as we walked out to the parking lot. I'd been at Greater Faith for a month now. Simone and I had worked ourselves into this comfortable routine of cleaning up the choir room after everyone else left, then walking out to our cars together.

Just like the last time, Simone laughed.

"What's so funny?" I asked.

"I am not a songwriter."

"How can you say that? You took 'Through it All' and 'Keep Moving' to a whole other level."

She leaned against her car and pressed her purse to her chest. "That's a bit of an exaggeration, don't you think?"

The way Simone tilted her head, and the way the lights in the parking lot shone on her face, made my heart kinda skip. I coughed, trying to shake that feeling away.

"Why . . ." I had to stop and clear my throat. "Why are you belittling your contribution to the song?"

She shrugged and, for the first time, I saw something cloud her eyes. What was it? Fear? Disappointment? Maybe it was lack of confidence, but that was weird because this girl had to know that she was all that.

I said, "Well, let me tell you what I think. You're more than a great singer. I think if you give yourself a chance, you'd be a terrific writer, too. So you might as well just give in, 'cause we are going to write this song together."

Again, she laughed, as if she wasn't taking a word that I was saying seriously. "Is that so?"

"Yup." I leaned against the car next to her. "And not only that. We're gonna write it and then we're gonna sing it together."

"A duet?" she asked. The laughter was gone from her tone now.

"Yeah. You don't have a problem singing with me, do you?"

"No, not at all. I'm just surprised, that's all."

"Why?"

"'Cause I don't know if anyone ever told you, but you can sing!" She laughed again.

"And you can too."

Once again, her laughter went away.

I said, "Simone, you do know that you can sing, right?"

She looked down at the ground, and kicked a stone away from her car when she nodded.

I frowned. This girl really didn't know what kind of talent she was carrying around. "Let me ask you something, Miss Simone."

She was still looking down, but I could see the ends of her lips curl, and I was glad that I'd made her smile again.

I asked, "You've never once considered being a singer?"

It took her a moment, but she finally looked up. Her eyes were glazed, and, for a moment, I thought she'd gone far away, someplace deep inside of herself. It was the way she just stared and didn't answer that made me think this.

Then, I repeated my question.

And I was shocked when she said, "I've done a lot more than think about it. Being a singer is my dream!"

Chapter 11

This was not a date. But for some reason, as I was getting ready, it sure felt like one. Especially with the way Chyanne was fussin' all over me.

"Now see, aren't you glad I came over here?" Chyanne said as she ran the flat iron through my hair one last time.

"I could've done this all by myself," I grumbled, though I was *mucho* grateful that Chyanne had shown up. I hadn't even called her, but Skye did. My big sister had to go to New York for some kind of interview, and, after I had called and told her about the talk Jaylen and I had, she'd called Chyanne and told her not to let me get ready for my date all by myself.

"You can act like a punk all you want," Chyanne said as she wrapped the cord around the flat iron, "but I know that deep down you're glad that I'm here."

I smiled at my sister-friend through the mirror. "Okay, deep, deep, deep down," I said.

And then, for no reason, we started giggling.

"Girl," Chyanne began, "I cannot believe you are going out on a date with that fine minister."

"It's not a date," I insisted. "And I don't think you should ever put the word 'fine' in front of the word 'minister.'"

"Why not?" she asked. "There are plenty of fine ministers walking this earth, thank you, Jesus!"

"Chyanne!"

"What? Tell the truth, shame the devil!"

She laughed, and I did too. Not because that was so funny,

but because it sounded like something Skye, and not Chyanne, would say.

"Well, whatever, this is not a date. Minister Jaylen and I are just going out to discuss some ideas he has for the song we're writing together."

"Mm-hmm."

"We are!"

"And he had to invite you to Maggiano's to discuss a song? Please!" Chyanne waved her hand in the air as if she were trying to get rid of my words. "You two could have just sat in the choir room and come up with a song if that's all this was about."

This time I waved my hand as if Chyanne was wrong, but my girl was just saying what I'd been thinking. Why did Minister Jaylen ask me to go with him to dinner? But then I shook my head, wanting to get that stupid question and any other stupid thoughts right out of my head. He probably just wanted us to go to someplace different, someplace nice, to get our creative juices going. I'd heard that a lot of artists went to different places to get fresh inspiration. So I needed to just keep my thoughts right there before I got my feelings hurt.

"Whatever!" I said, glancing at myself in the mirror once again. I looked okay; I was wearing black, and everyone said that black was slimming. But was this slimming enough?

There was a loud knock on my door, but before I could open it, Devin sashayed in.

"What are you doing here?" I asked him, even though I was looking at Chyanne suspiciously. I was gonna kill her if she'd told Devin that I had a date.

"I cannot believe you heifers were going to do all of this without telling me!" His hands moved with a flourish, as if he were conducting some kind of symphony. "Your first date in ages, and you were going to try to keep it a secret from a brother."

"It's not a date!" I said, rolling my eyes at him and Chyanne. "I didn't tell you because I didn't want you making a big deal out of nothing."

"Mm-hmm," he hummed, just like Chyanne had done to me a little while before.

Devin looked me up and down with critical eyes, and his expression—eyebrows furrowed and lips just as tight—made me want to call Jaylen and tell him to forget about it.

"What's wrong?" I whined.

"Oh, not a thing," Devin said, finally grinning. "You look fab. But how would you like to go from fab to fab-u-lous?" He didn't even give me a chance to answer before he pulled some kind of black contraption out of his bag. "Voila!"

He laughed and I frowned. "What is this?"

"It's magic, girl. Body Magic."

Then, as he tossed another garment to Chyanne, he explained how, by putting on this thing, I was going to look two to three sizes smaller. "So, what are you? An eighteen?" he asked.

I answered him by rolling my eyes. A man was never supposed to ask a lady her dress size. Didn't he know the rules? But then again, it wasn't like Devin was playing for the male team. Plus, how could I be mad when he'd guessed my size right on the nose?

He said, "So once you put this on, you'll look as if you're wearing a fourteen, or maybe even a twelve."

Okay, I may have been upset with Devin for being in my business, but all of my mad was gone now. This thing could make me look like I was a size twelve? I hadn't worn a twelve since I was in kindergarten.

I snatched the contraption out of his hands and dashed into the bathroom.

"Wait," Devin yelled. "You're gonna need help."

Help? Please! I was a grown woman; what kind of woman needed help getting into a foundation garment?

Five minutes later, I yelled out for Chyanne. And five minutes after that, she begged Devin to come into the bathroom too. But fifteen minutes after I first walked in, I shimmied back into my dress, and then I stepped out of the bathroom to applause.

"OMG!" I exclaimed.

As Chyanne and Devin clapped, they were saying the same thing.

"You look . . ." Chyanne began.

Devin finished, "Fab-u-lous! Didn't I tell you?"

"Where did you get this thing?" I asked.

"I'm selling them," he said proudly. "I'm a distributor."

"Well, I want one," Chyanne said, as she ran her hands through my hair to flatten the strands that had come out of place. "But, first, we've got to get you out of here," she said to me. "You're gonna be late."

I glanced at the clock. How did it get to be six thirty already? My plan had been to leave five minutes ago so that I could get over to Maggiano's about five minutes after Jaylen, who was always on time. But it was hard to get moving now. I couldn't stop staring at myself in the mirror, and I couldn't remember the last time that had happened.

"Okay, I'm ready," I said, right before I grabbed the matching jacket from the bed.

Devin moaned. "Why are you going to ruin that fantastic dress with that?"

I frowned. "The dress came with this jacket."

"But you don't need it," Chyanne said. "The jacket hides all of your curves."

Glancing in the mirror again, I could see that she was right. "But what am I supposed to do about my arms?" I whined.

"What's wrong with your arms?"

I looked at Chyanne. For someone so smart, that was the dumbest question I'd ever heard. "My arms are fat!"

Devin said, "And so you think by hiding your arms, no one will know they're fat?"

First, he'd asked me my size, and now, he was saying that I had fat arms. I mean, I did have fat arms, but he wasn't supposed to say that. On any other day, my feelings would have been really hurt. But I looked too good right now to go out like that.

Maybe Devin was trying to make it up to me, maybe not. But he said, "Look, all I'm sayin' is that your arms are your arms. No matter what you put on, everyone knows their size. So be bold and be proud!" he cheered.

I slipped off the jacket, but, even though I looked tight in the dress, I still wasn't feeling it. "You don't have any magic for these?" I said, flapping my arms as if they were wings.

Devin and Chyanne laughed.

"Nope," he said. "But, I'm telling you, you look good, girl. And you know me; my mama should have named me The Truth."

I glanced back at Chyanne, leaning against the wall with her arms folded. With a grin, she nodded like she agreed with everything Devin was saying.

"Okay," I said, tossing the jacket onto the bed.

My friends clapped.

"Now let's go," Chyanne said, grabbing my purse from the desk.

With a final glance, I raced out of my room with my friends right behind me. But by the time I got to the elevator, I'd changed my mind.

"Hold it when it gets here," I said to Devin and Chyanne before I dashed back down the hall to my room. I had to get my jacket.

Chapter 12

I sprayed one last squirt of Issey Miyake onto my neck, and then I stepped into the hallway and right into Miles.

"Whoa," he said, as he backed up and looked me up and down. "Where're you going?"

"Out."

"Come on, 'fess up," he said. "With that suit and that grin, there's more going on than you just going out."

Okay, my boy had me. Not that there was anything to tell. I was going out, but it wasn't a date or anything. I just wanted to get out with Simone and talk, not only about our song, but about her dreams to become a singer. And I'd wanted a special place to tell her that I was about to make all of her dreams come true.

"I'm gonna hook up with Simone."

His eyes got wide. "Simone. Really? I didn't know you were hanging like that with Simone."

Right then, Quintin came around the corner from his bedroom. "You mean fat girl Simone?" he asked, jumping right into the middle of our conversation.

I could not believe that he'd said that. And from the scowl on Miles's face, neither could he.

"What?" Quintin asked as we stared him down. "Don't tell me you never noticed that the floor shakes with every step she takes." He laughed.

We didn't.

"That's not even funny, man," I said, shaking my head.

Miles added, "Yeah, that's not right."

Quintin shrugged. He said, "I'm sorry," though there was not a semblance of an apology inside his tone.

I turned to Miles. "Yeah, Simone and I are going to dinner," I said, ignoring Quintin. "We need to talk over a few things."

Miles nodded.

I had turned my back to Quintin, giving him the chance to just walk away. But my frat brother didn't know how to do that.

"Dinner? I hope you're taking her to an all-you-can-eat buffet since you don't have a real job." It was only after he got those last words in that he decided to step. We could still hear his chuckles as he trotted down the stairs. "Man, I crack myself up," he said, before I heard the front door close.

It must've been the way I was glaring that made Miles say, "I know you're not trippin' on that fool."

"Nah, nah, I'm not."

"'Cause, from what you've told me, Simone's a nice girl."

"She is, but it's not even like that. We're just going to talk."

Miles glanced at me from the corner of his eye before he laughed. "Yeah, right." He held out his fist to give me dap.

Glancing at my watch, I turned toward the stairs. "I'm out," I told Miles as I rushed down to the first floor. As I grabbed the keys, I was still a bit bothered by what Quintin had said. But, on the real, he was just being Quintin. If he weren't my frat, and if he weren't part of Tru Harmony . . .

But what bothered me more was the way Miles looked at me. And the way he laughed. As if he didn't believe that this wasn't a date.

I shook my head. I didn't know why I was trippin' on Miles. I needed to keep my head on one thing, and that was this talk with Simone. I didn't need to be thinking about Quintin or Miles. This was all about Simone and Tru Harmony—nothing more, nothing less.

Chapter 13

I know I looked crazy, sitting on my hands in this classy restaurant. But it was the only way I could stop them from shaking. The truth was I was nervous as all get-out, and I didn't really know why. I mean, it wasn't like this was a date. We were just two friends getting together to talk, right? So why did I start shaking the moment I saw Jaylen?

When I pulled up in front of the restaurant, he was already standing there, waiting for me. He came to my car before the valet attendant could make a move.

"Hey, you," he said as he opened my door.

That was when I started shaking. It was because of the way he took my hand and held on to me as the attendant gave him the ticket for my car. Our hands were still together as he led me into the restaurant.

Lord, please don't let my palms start to sweat, I prayed. I mean, nothing would have been more embarrassing than that. Then, I began to think about trippin' on the carpet and falling on my face. Now *that* would have been beyond humiliating.

But even when I'd made it to the table without sweating or tripping, I couldn't stop shaking.

"Are you all right?" Jaylen asked me once the hostess walked away after seating us.

"Yeah," I said. I could feel that stupid grin on my face. The one I always wore when I was nervous. "I'm cool. What about you?" I asked, because I didn't know what else to say.

"I'm fine."

Through the flickering light that came from the single candle in the middle of the table, his face had this gorgeous bronze glow that made him look like he should have been modeling in a magazine or something. Then, Jaylen smiled, and I couldn't do anything but relax. Slowly, I lifted my hands and rested them on the table.

He said, "You look really nice, Simone." A moment passed before he added, "I know you hear this a lot, but you really got it going on. You're one beautiful young lady."

It took everything I had not to shake my head and tell him that no, I didn't hear that a lot. All I ever heard were comments like, "You have such a pretty face," or "You're kinda cute for a big girl." But Jaylen was always talking to me and looking at me like he didn't notice that I wasn't a size six. He almost made me want to pull off my jacket and show him what I was really working with, since I had on this Body Magic. But I wasn't crazy enough to do that.

Jaylen looked at me like he was waiting for me to respond to what he'd said about me being beautiful. But all I did was turn my head from one side to the other, and look around at all the white clothed tables around us that were decorated with their own candles. "Have you been here before?"

Jaylen chuckled as if he knew that I was dodging his compliment, but I figured I'd asked him a good enough question to get away with that. I mean, this was a really nice restaurant, and kind of expensive, too. I wondered how Jaylen had heard about it, since he'd just been in Atlanta for a little over a month.

"Nah," he said as he flicked his napkin in the air and then set it on his lap. I did the same thing. "But it comes highly recommended. So, what are you going to have?" he asked as he picked up his menu.

I glanced at mine and my eyes bugged at the prices. Although I ate out with Skye, Chyanne, and Devin all the time, we usually stayed away from places that didn't give us back change from a twenty.

"Have anything you want," Jaylen said. "I heard the lasagna is good. And, of course, chicken is good no matter where you go."

I moved my eyes away from those entrees and studied the salads and appetizers. "I think I'll have the Mediterranean chicken salad," I said, since it was one of the least expensive items on the menu. It wasn't like I was about to pig out at Jaylen's expense.

He frowned. "That's it?"

"Uh-huh." I nodded and pushed my menu aside. "I'm not really hungry." Right at that moment, my stomach growled as if it were calling me a liar. I put my hand over my mouth, coughed, and prayed that Jaylen hadn't heard that.

After our waiter took our orders and walked away, Jaylen got straight to the point. "So, you've been dreaming about becoming a singer." He shook his head. "I never would have known that."

"Why?"

"'Cause you never mentioned it. I mean, everyone talks about being a singer. Even people who can't *sang*," he said, purposely using the wrong word, "want to be *sangers*." He laughed as if he'd just told the biggest joke. "So, why were you keeping that on the down low?"

I shrugged. "I wasn't keeping it a secret," I said, thinking about how many times I'd talked about my dreams with my sister and my friends.

"Could've fooled me," he said. "So, how bad do you want it?"

That was a question that I didn't expect, and it took me a moment to think of an answer. Though I got all As in English and had an extensive vocabulary, I couldn't think of any words to truly describe how badly I wanted to be a singer.

"Really badly," was all I could think to say. "But I can't see it happening."

I expected him to ask me why not. But he just grinned. "I can make it happen for you."

I frowned; that was my cue for him to explain.

He did. "I want you to be the first artist on the Tru Harmony label."

"Tru Harmony?" I'd never heard of them. But then, Jaylen explained that this was his company, a label he was starting with his boys. I sat back in my seat, shocked. I guess we both had secrets.

"That's why I'm here in Atlanta," he said.

My eyes were wide as he told me how they expected to become as big as So So Def or Jazzy Pha's label Sho'nuff. "But the thing is, we have to come out smokin'. We have to come out with the right artist."

Even as the waiter brought us our food, Jaylen kept on talking. While he ate, he explained how his frat brother, Quintin, was the brains behind the business, while Miles was the IT guy.

"And I'm in charge of all things creative," Jaylen said. "The music, the artists. So now, let's get back to the question: do you want to be a singer?"

At least thirty minutes had passed since Jaylen had started talking, and all I'd had to do was listen and dream. But now came the moment when I had to talk—and tell the truth. It took me a moment to say honestly, "I'll never be a singer."

If we had been in a balloon, we would have dropped straight to the ground, because it was like my words had taken all the air out of the room.

Jaylen said, "But I thought you said this was your dream."

"Well, dreams and reality are two different things." I guessed it was time to come clean all the way. So I told Jaylen about my father.

He listened like he really cared, never interrupting me as I explained what my father's dream was for me. "Singing is totally out as far as my dad is concerned."

"I think your father's just trying to protect you."

"That's what he says."

"But the game is different now," Jaylen said. I didn't know what game he was talking about until he explained, "Your father's concerned because he knows how many people are out there who are great singers but who never get signed. He's just afraid that you'll put in all of this work but never get a deal." Jaylen stopped and leaned forward a bit. "But Tru Harmony changes everything. We're gonna give you that deal; we're gonna make you a star!"

I sat quietly, just taking in everything that Jaylen said. And his words made a lot of sense. There were thousands upon thousands of singers who were trying to make it and my dad knew this. But if I was already signed to a label . . .

"So you think . . ."

I didn't even get a chance to finish before Jaylen said, "I *know* that's what's bothering your father. Look, if you were my daughter, I'd protect you too." He leaned forward a little, and his face was once again right in front of the candlelight. "So, Simone Davenport, just say the word and you'll make me one happy business owner."

"Yes." I whispered at first, but then I yelled out, "Yes," so loudly, other people in the restaurant started looking at us.

Jaylen laughed before he reached across the table and squeezed my hand. "That's the word!"

My thoughts were tumbling inside my head as Jaylen called for the waiter and asked for the check. I was about to have a recording contract! Like a real singer. My dream was coming true. Just the thought of that gave me goosebumps.

"So, are you ready to get out of here?"

I was so deep inside my thoughts that I didn't even notice that Jaylen had not only already paid the bill, but he was standing up, waiting for me to join him. I scooted out of my chair, and, just like when we came into the restaurant, Jaylen held my hand as he led the way.

He gave my ticket to the attendant and, as we waited, he said, "It's going to take a few weeks for the contracts to be drawn up, but I don't see why we have to wait. Quintin and Miles are as eager as I am to get started, so if you don't mind working even though we don't have all the legal stuff in place, we can get this thing moving."

"No, I don't mind," I said, not really knowing what he meant.

"Great! Then let's get into the studio. I already have a couple of songs that I want you to look at. If we can find one that you want to work with, we can get started, so that by the time the contracts are ready and all parties have checked everything out, we can just pop out your first single."

Okay, this was serious. Jaylen wasn't just talking about something that was down the road. He was talking contracts, and studios, and singles. He was talking about now!

I nodded because I just didn't have the words. Was this really happening to me?

My car rolled up, and Jaylen slipped the attendant a tip, then stood by the door. But just as I was about to get inside, he leaned forward and kissed me on the cheek. He kept his lips on my skin for a moment, and even when he pulled away, I could still feel him. I looked up with shock in my eyes. But there wasn't even a little bit of surprise on his face. Jaylen just grinned as if kissing me were the most normal thing in the world.

"Good night, Miss Tru Harmony," he said right before he closed the door.

I waved, but didn't say a word. How could I? My mind was so crowded with thoughts that I couldn't figure out how to speak. I wasn't sure what had my attention more: the contract or the kiss. But then, I came back to earth and realized the kiss was probably because of the contract.

The contract! I was going to be a real singer, with a real deal. All of a sudden, I leaned my head back and screamed so loud the windows vibrated. My dream was finally coming true, and in a way my father couldn't possibly have a problem with.

But thinking about my father took just a little bit of the joy away. What Jaylen had said about my dad made sense, but I didn't want to take any chances. I wasn't going to say a word to my father . . . at least, not yet. But there was not a thing that was gonna stop me from telling Skye. And Chyanne and Devin.

I couldn't wait to get back to my dorm.

Chapter 14

"Man, I heard her sing! That girl can blow," Miles said right after I told him my plan of making Simone our lead artist.

"So, you think it's a good idea?"

He nodded. "I mean, I'm no judge of talent . . . that's your gig. But I got ears, and from what I hear, she's as good as any of those females on the other labels. Maybe even better, 'cause she sounds like she has the range of Mariah."

I couldn't stop grinning. I knew Miles would love the idea of Simone. But now, I had to ask him to do something that I wasn't sure he'd be down to do.

"Just one thing," I said, my smile totally gone now. I was looking down at the mixing console, wanting to keep my next words as casual as possible. "Don't say anything about Simone to Quintin."

By the sound of Miles's voice, I knew he was frowning. "Why not? I thought we were making all of these decisions together."

Finally, I looked at Miles. "Yeah, we are. And, I'm gonna tell him. Just . . . not yet." When his frown deepened, I explained, "I want to have Simone ready as a total package before I bring in Q."

Miles shook his head as if he had no idea what I was talking about.

"I want to present her to Quintin as a complete artist, with the right song and the right look. I'm gonna get a stylist to work with her . . . you know . . . "

In an instant, Miles got what I was saying. The way he squint-ed, I could tell that he was remembering the mean statements Quintin had made about Simone.

"I have a plan," I assured Miles. "By the time I bring Sim-one to Quintin, she'll be so tight, so ready, he'll be her biggest fan."

He nodded. "Sounds like a good idea."

My grin was back.

Miles turned toward the stairs, but then he came back. "Let me ask you something." He paused. "You're not catching feel-ings for this girl, are you?"

"Nah," I said, shaking my head hard. "Why would you ask me that?"

He shrugged. "I don't know. First, you had dinner with her yesterday—"

"That was just to talk about picking her up."

"And now today, you're gonna make her a star."

"You and Quintin have been waiting for me; I'm just deliver-ing."

"A'ight," he said, responding to my explanations. "It's just that . . ." He stopped. "Getting involved with her wouldn't be a good idea."

"I know that."

"We've got to keep this all strictly business."

"That's all she is to me," I insisted. "As far as females go, she's not even my type."

He chuckled. "Man, you don't have a type. If we went down the list of all the girls—"

I held up my hand. "You got me mixed up with Q, man. I ain't been with a bunch of females."

"You know what I'm sayin'." Miles was still laughing a bit. But then he got serious. "I mean it, man. Let's keep this clean. No getting involved with the talent."

"You got it," I said before Miles trotted up the stairs and out of the studio. I didn't mind my boy talking to me about Simone like that. I mean, that's how we rolled. Always straight, always with truth.

But Miles didn't need to trip on this. Simone was a nice girl and everything, but this was all about Tru Harmony. Straight-up business. And it wasn't going to be difficult to keep it that way because Simone wasn't interested in me either. She was always professional, friendly, but distant. Anyway, as fine as she was, she probably had a Morehouse man, maybe even a couple of them on speed dial.

That thought made me feel a little bad, but just for a moment. The only thing I wanted on my mind was Tru Harmony. And how me and my boys were finally on our way.

Chapter 15

When the bell rang, I dashed to the door and swung it open. "Why didn't you use your key?" I asked my sister.

Skye looked around before she stepped inside the house. "I don't have a key," she said. "You must've forgotten that Daddy made me give mine back."

I had forgotten that, but I hadn't forgotten that it had been forever since Skye had been home. Even now, I couldn't believe that she had really shown up. It had taken a bit of convincing, but this was why I loved my big sister—she always came through for me.

"You're sure they're not going to show up anytime soon?" Skye asked as she took slow steps from the foyer into the living room.

"I'm sure," I said, following her inside. "That's why I'm here. Mom asked me to wait for the plumber to come because she had a Ladies Auxiliary planning meeting and Daddy had to go to Macon." I had already told Skye this, but I knew she needed to hear it again.

My sister stood in the middle of the living room, like she was trying to decide if she should stay or make a quick getaway. I took a deep breath, and said a little prayer. When she dumped her bag onto the sofa, I exhaled.

Slowly, she glanced around the living room. "Wow."

"What's wrong?"

"I haven't been here in a minute."

"I know," I said, thinking that it had been over three years—

before she graduated from college—since Skye had been home. "But nothing's changed." I plopped down onto the couch and waited for her to join me.

"That's the point; not a thing has changed." Skye strolled in front of the fireplace, taking in all the photos. "Everything's the same, yet so much is different." There were dozens of pictures on the mantel, chronicling our lives from childhood to where we were now. Skye stood still, staring at the photos as if she was remembering. "I'm surprised Daddy didn't burn every piece of paper that had my face on it."

"He wouldn't do that."

Finally, she sat next to me. "He might as well have. It's not as if he considers me a Davenport anymore."

I frowned. Her voice was so low, so sad, like she was really hurt by what had gone down between her and our dad. All of this time, I thought Skye wasn't fazed by it at all. She always acted so strong, as if all that mattered was what she wanted to do. In spite of our father, she'd pursued her dream and made herself a success, even without our parent's approval. I didn't think she needed anybody's support, not with how she'd left and never looked back. But the way she sounded today made me wonder. I guessed, like our dad, she was hurt too.

"Why don't you try to talk to Daddy?" I asked. "I mean, it's been years. Enough time has passed."

She shook her head. "I'm not about to have him hang up on me or throw me out of his house." Her strong, stubborn voice was back.

I nodded. When Skye first moved to New York, she had called over and over again. But our dad just kept telling her that he didn't want to talk to her. That she'd made her decision and now he'd made his. It seemed so childish to me, but I was not going to be the one to tell the great Reverend Davenport that he wasn't acting age appropriate. Honestly, I thought my mom would tell him to start acting like the adult, but I guess she didn't want to be the one to correct him either.

"Anyway, I don't want to stay here too long," Skye said, glancing over her shoulder at the front door. "So, what's up? What's this big news that you just had to tell me in person?"

After I had left Jaylen, I had planned to tell Skye the moment I got to my dorm. But when I got home and thought about it, I knew this news was too big to tell over the telephone. So, I'd called Skye and asked to meet her. It killed me to have to wait three days, but this was the first time that Skye could get away.

I had this big plan to drag out the news, and make Skye beg me to tell her. But it was just busting out of me. I scooted closer to her on the couch. "I got a recording contract!"

"What?"

"A recording contract. I'm gonna be a singer for real."

"Oh my God!" Skye hugged me. Then she sat back as I told her all the details. "Wow!" she said, when I finished filling her in on everything Jaylen had shared with me. "This is wonderful."

"You really think so?"

She nodded. "Yeah, of course. How could it be anything but wonderful?"

I shrugged. "I don't know. I didn't know what you would think of Tru Harmony since it isn't really a company; I mean, not a big company."

She waved her hand in the air like that didn't matter. "Unless you have the chance to work with Clive Davis, this kind of situation is off the chain."

"Really?" That's what I felt, but it was great to have my big sister saying exactly what I was thinking.

She nodded. "Because people like Jaylen and his boys are hungry. They're gonna make it happen for you because if you're successful, then they are too. Simone, I am so happy for you!" She wrapped her arms around me again.

Having my sister's approval took my excitement level up one

hundred notches. Not able to sit down any longer, I jumped from the couch and paced in front of her. Part of my energy was from my exhilaration, but, now, the anxiety was settling in.

"Okay," I began, still filled with too much energy to stop walking. "How do I tell Daddy?"

That wiped the smile right off her face. "Are you sure you want to tell him?"

"How can I not? It's not like I can keep this a secret. I mean if I do this, I may not be able to take the job with Ernst & Young."

Skye moaned. "If you don't take that job, Daddy's gonna kick you out of his life for sure."

"But I'll have a contract," I whined.

Skye sat back and crossed her legs like she was totally calm. But while she was cool and collected, my blood pressure was rising off the charts.

"Yeah, you'll have a contract . . . just like I had a job," she said. "But that won't matter to Daddy. If you're not doing exactly what he wants you to do, if he's not in control of your life, then he won't want to have anything to do with you."

I shook my head, not really wanting to believe her. "But this might be different," I said. "I mean, Daddy's known that I wanted to be a singer all my life."

"And he knew that I wanted to be a designer. What does what you want to do have to do with anything? Trust and know, he will kick you out of his life."

I fell back onto the couch, all of my excitement and energy gone.

"This is never going to happen for me, is it?" It was a question, but I didn't expect an answer. "I'm never going to be a singer. Daddy's not going to let me do this."

"It's not up to him."

"But you just said . . ."

"This is *your* life."

Yeah, that was the truth, but it didn't really mean anything. It wasn't like I could do what Skye had done. I couldn't just walk away knowing that my father would be so disappointed. I couldn't walk away knowing that my father would feel like both of his daughters had deserted him.

I wasn't strong like Skye. Disappointing my father would kill me as much as it would kill him.

"People don't get chances like this," Skye said as if she knew that I needed to be reminded of that. "You've wanted to do this your whole life, and you may never get this chance again."

I nodded; but how was I going to work this out? Maybe I could convince my father that God had brought this opportunity to me because, truly, that was the way I felt.

"I've got to get going." Skye stood up and hoisted her purse onto her shoulder. I didn't really think she had anywhere to go, since she'd told me that she'd taken off the whole morning. She had probably just stayed in our parents' house for as long as she could.

Skye hugged me. "You've got to go after this, Monnie," she said. It had been years since Skye had called me by the name she'd made up for me when we were kids. She hardly ever called me that now, and hearing her say it made me want to cry.

"Call me later," she said before she walked out of the door, leaving me with thoughts of how I wished I could be more like her. Because if I were, this would be a no-brainer. This would be all about me, and my dad would just have to find a way to handle it.

But I wasn't anything like Skye, I was just Simone. Still, I was gonna find a way to work this out. I just had to.

Chapter 16

Today was the day. A week exactly to the day when I'd told Simone that I was gonna make her a star. Finally, we were taking the first steps to making her dream, and mine, come true.

For the last seven days we had worked our butts off, spending every free hour we had together. It was amazing the way we flowed, as if we had always been friends. I would start saying something and Simone would finish my sentence. Simone would be thinking something and I would say it out loud. It was like she was the other half of me, knowing exactly where I was going all the time. And what I loved was that she didn't have a diva complex; this wasn't just about her. Simone cared about Tru Harmony as much as I did, talking to and encouraging me all the time about the direction of the company.

"I want us to stand out," I told Simone. "Every single one of our singers is going to have something special. That's why I'm so glad you're the first."

"I'm the one who's honored," she said to me. "I have no doubt that with you at the head, Tru Harmony is going to be one of the biggest labels in the country!"

My head got big sometimes with the things she said. But our talks weren't just about me and Tru Harmony. I was just as interested in Simone's life. That's why I'd told her to take the job with that accounting firm when she graduated.

"It'll just be for a little while; that'll be your cushion, 'cause we're not gonna be able to pay you any kind of advance. But we'll make up for it with higher royalties, and, within a year, you'll be rollin' in it, baby!"

Without hesitation, Simone had agreed with me. It was just like that with us—easy. We could talk about anything and laugh about everything. Though there was one subject where there was little talking and definitely no laughing: Reverend Davenport. I'd tried to tap into what was happening on the home front between Simone and her father, but that was one place where she wouldn't let me in. I didn't even know if the two of them had ever talked about Simone and Tru Harmony, but after a while I decided that I really didn't need to know. Once we got Simone going, no one—not even her father—would want to stand in the way of success.

I had so many thoughts going on inside my head that I didn't hear the doorbell ring.

"Yo, J! You got company," Miles yelled just before Simone came down the stairs.

I saw her first, and then I saw the female with her. But even though I wondered about her partner (because Simone had never brought anyone with her before), I put those thoughts aside for a minute, 'cause my girl was looking fine. There was no doubt that a lot of guys might consider Simone a big girl, but what they were missing was an appreciation of a woman with curves, something that gave me great pleasure. Because nobody, I mean, nobody, could rock boobs and booty like a black woman. And Simone was rocking it all the way in her white shirt and skinny jeans.

I took my mind out of the gutter and said, "What's up?" to Simone just before I kissed her cheek.

The other female raised one eyebrow and, as soon as she did that, I knew this was Skye, Simone's sister. I didn't understand why I didn't see that right away. I mean, the two looked like twins, really, from the maple hue of their skin, to their bushy eyebrows and heart-shaped lips. The only real difference was that Skye was smaller than Simone; the big sister didn't have the same banging body as the little sister.

I'd met Simone's best friends, Chyanne and Devin, a couple of times, but I'd never caught up with Skye, even though Simone talked about her sister all the time. Holding out my hand, I said, "It's nice to meet you, Skye. Finally."

Skye grinned. "Nice to meet you too."

Simone said, "How did you know this was my sister?"

"Are you kidding me?" I laughed. Turning to Skye, I added, "I'm glad you came."

Simone said, "I hope you don't mind."

"Nah, nah," I said, making a final adjustment on the console. "It's cool. I want you to have all the support you need. So, Skye," I began. I didn't know why I felt the need to impress Simone's sister, but I really wanted her to like me. "What do you think of all of this?"

"What? About my sister becoming a superstar?" Her grin showed just how proud she was of Simone. "It's fantastic," she said, and then motioned toward the big chair that we had pushed into the corner.

I nodded, but said, "You can sit there, or you can join me here."

She shook her head as she looked at the stool that was next to me. "No, this is fine. I don't want to be in the way."

I wasn't going to argue, since I was trying to make a good impression and everything. When I turned to Simone, she smiled, and my heart kinda took an extra beat. I wasn't sure where that came from. It was probably just my nerves. I mean, this was huge. This was the beginning of everything that we'd both dreamed of.

Taking an extra breath, I said, "Okay, let's get this party started." I turned all of my attention to my protégé—at least, that's what I liked to call her. "You ready to do this?"

The way Simone nodded and then turned toward the booth let me know that she was definitely ready. But, though she acted all confident, I would've bet that she'd been up half the night, anxious, exactly the way I'd been.

For a week we'd written lyrics, debated melodies, adjusted tempos. We had worked until we couldn't work anymore. Worked until we had the perfect song.

So, both of us were ready.

Even though Simone had never done this before, I didn't have to tell her much. She was a natural, the way she walked into the booth and slipped the headphones over her ears. When she nodded at me through the glass, I sat down at the console, forgetting all about Skye. It was just me and my girl.

"Ready, kiddo?" I spoke to her through the mic.

She nodded.

I turned on the track, and, after the first few bars of the verse, Simone began to sing.

"I'm the dream maker. Like a genie in a bottle, three wishes, boy, you got it. I'm the dream maker. I'll do anything for you, I can make all your dreams come true."

I didn't know what Simone was doing, but this sounded better than any of the one hundred times we'd rehearsed.

It took everything in me to focus on the controls, because all I wanted to do was sit back and listen. This was really happening!

"What the."

I held up my hand as Miles trotted down the stairs. Even though he was home, I hadn't told him that we were recording. I worked in the basement studio all the time without Miles or Quintin coming down. My hope that they would both stay away today. I was sure that Quintin would, he was never home on Saturdays. But I knew there was a chance that Miles would hear us. Not that it mattered—with the way Simone sounded, I knew my frat would be on board all the way now.

Miles stood behind me, staring through the glass, as mesmerized by Simone as I was. I had planned to take this song bar by bar, verse by verse, stopping and starting until it was just right. But I wasn't about to stop, not with the way Simone was nailing it. Was this even possible? Could we have the perfect single with only one try?

When Simone threw back her head, closed her eyes, and hit that last note, holding it far longer than the track, all I could do was sit there. I wasn't the only one captivated; neither Miles nor Skye moved either.

Finally, Simone stood straight and opened her eyes. It was like it took a moment for her to come back to earth, and, when she did, she frowned, staring back at the three of us who were staring at her. Tossing off her headphones, she said, "What's wrong?"

Wrong? It was obvious that babygirl couldn't hear herself, because if she could, there was no way the word "wrong" would have come out of her mouth.

I turned on the mic. "Nothing. It's all good."

She shrugged a little. "I'm gonna do that again, okay? I know I can do better."

"Better?" Miles whispered. "It can't possibly get any better than that."

Miles was right; Simone had stepped straight into it, all the way, the first time out. But I nodded anyway. I wanted—no, I needed—to again hear her sing those words that we'd written together.

"Okay," Simone said. She stood in the booth with a wide stance, like she was buckling down, ready to give it her all, as if she hadn't already done that.

Then Simone started again. And just like she promised, it was better. No way that was possible, but I was listening with my own ears. The words slipped through her lips like silk and glided around us, massaging our ears. Somehow, she'd turned the song into a dream, and she pulled us into her trance. This was amazing to watch and even more astonishing to listen to. I'd heard many sing—Whitney, Janet, Mariah—but there was something about Simone, a depth that resonated inside my soul. It was as if she'd taken the best from each of the greats. She had Whitney's grit and Janet's sweetness and Mariah's range all in one voice.

"Who the heck is that?"

If I hadn't been so captivated, I would have been upset by hearing Quintin. But I didn't have to worry anymore about what he would think. Because now that he heard Simone, there wouldn't be a damn thing he would say. Quintin was a lot of things, but he was no dummy. It was clear that Simone was going to be a star.

Through the mirror's reflection, I saw Quintin ease up behind me and peer into the booth. The smile he'd brought downstairs was gone when he saw Simone, but then his attention turned to Skye.

"What's up, beautiful one," Quintin said.

I was just about to motion to him to be quiet, when Skye did it for me.

"I'm listening to my sister," she said, waving Quintin away, even as her eyes stayed on the recording booth.

But there had never been a female, or a male for that matter, who'd ever been able to shut Quintin up.

"That's *your* sister?"

Skye's forehead creased with wrinkles. She squinted. "Please!" she exclaimed, though her mouth hardly moved. That was as polite a "be quiet" that Quintin was going to get.

Quintin did shut up, but only for the moment. Without an invitation, he rested on the arm of the chair where Skye sat. She moved to the edge, but that didn't bother my brother. Quintin stayed, staring at Skye now, while Skye just kept watching Simone.

Then, Simone hit that last note again. This time, she made all of us, including Quintin, stand up like we were at a concert or something.

Miles and I clapped as Skye pushed past us. Simone hadn't

taken one step out of the booth before her sister was all over her.

"Oh my God. You were wonderful," Skye cried.

"So it was okay?" she asked. The question was supposed to be for Skye, but Simone was looking straight at me.

Okay? Please! I wanted to give her my own hug, but I stood back as Skye held on to her sister like she planned to never let her go.

"You were great," I said.

"So, I don't have to do it again?"

"There's no way you could do it any better." This time, it was Miles who reassured her. "Trust me, you were off the charts the first time. And what you just did . . ." Miles shook his head like he had no other words. "Trust me," he repeated, "you don't have to do it again." Then, he turned to me. "Am I right or am I right?"

I grinned. Without even knowing it, Miles had just given his approval for our first song.

I was basking in the celebration . . . and then I remembered Quintin. He was standing off to the side, leaning against the wall, with his arms crossed. He was smiling, but it had nothing to do with Simone. His eyes were on Skye—on Skye's butt, to be specific.

Oh, Lord! I hoped he wasn't going to try to hit that. Not that I thought he had a chance. I'd just met Skye, but I already knew that she wouldn't be impressed by Quintin's smooth talk and suave walk.

Simone grabbed her bag. "May I use your restroom?"

"Sure," Miles said. "I'll take you up."

"I'm going with you," Skye said, following the two.

I shook my head. With the way Simone had rocked that song, I wondered if we should record another one. Neither one of us had expected Simone's very first session to go this well, but since we had the time, I figured we should move forward. Hell, with the way we were going, I thought we might have a whole CD by the end of the day. That idea made me chuckle.

"So, what were you guys doing down here?"

My mind was so into the recording session that I'd forgotten about Quintin. Though I had wanted to wait until I had Simone ready as a whole package, there was no reason not to tell him now. He'd just heard her; there couldn't be any doubts that she was going to be a star.

"You just heard the first single that'll be released by Tru Harmony."

"What?"

I was so proud of my discovery that I wanted to beat my chest. "I signed Simone as our first artist." I grinned.

Quintin waved his hand in the air like he was trying to wipe away my words and my smile. "Man, you've got to be kidding me. You want to sign Simone?"

Okay, hadn't he just heard what I'd heard? "What's your problem, Q? You just heard her sing."

"Yeah, I heard her and I saw her. Have you looked at that girl?" he yelled.

"Bring it down," I warned with an edge in my voice. I was pissed. I couldn't believe that Quintin was coming out of his mouth like this. What did it matter that Simone wasn't some pencil-thin model type? She looked better than any of those anorexic-looking women on magazine covers. "There's nothing wrong with the way she looks," I whispered, not wanting Simone to hear any of this craziness.

"She's fat," he said.

I wanted to punch him just for saying that. But now that we were businessmen, I had to find a better way to handle our disagreements. "What does her dress size have to do with singing? She can rock any song." I paused so that he could remember what he'd just heard. "And she's gorgeous."

"She's fat," he repeated as if he was trying to drill that fact into my mind. "She may have a pretty face, but with that body she's unattractive and, therefore, ineligible. Now, her sister . . . What's her name?"

"Her sister's not a singer," I said, fighting to hold back my anger. There was no way I wanted Simone and Skye to come back down here and see the two of us duking it out, but this fool was about to take me there. "And, anyway, it's done. We're signing Simone."

"No. We're not. There's no way I'm gonna sign on to something that will make us the laughingstock of Atlanta."

I snapped. "What are you talking about!" Now, I was the one yelling. "There are plenty of big girls, gorgeous girls, who sing. Ever heard of Jennifer Hudson, Jill Scott—"

He didn't let me go on. "And for every one of those, there are a hundred girls who are right and tight."

For a second, I wondered how Quintin and I had ever become friends, because, right about now, I was embarrassed to even know anyone this ignorant.

"Man, we're the new kids on the block," Quintin kept on. "When we step out, we gotta step correct or we'll find ourselves right back in L.A. working for the man for the rest of our lives."

"So, you'd rather have some model in here who can't sing?"

"You don't have to know how to sing to be a singer. Not with all the equipment we have," he said, waving his hand over our studio. "We can fix anybody's voice."

"So, you just want a studio artist?" I said in a tone that would let him know that was ridiculous.

He shrugged. "As long as she looks good."

"What about concerts? Personal appearances?"

"She can lip-sync."

I shook my head. "We're not passing on Simone."

"What? You screwing her?"

My fingers curled, turning my hands into two tight fists.

He said, "Simone is never going to be part of Tru Harmony. She's too fat for us to put our name behind her."

Just when I was about to deck him, I heard the slow, soft tap of footsteps on the stairs. I froze, wanting to close my eyes and pray, but there was no need to bring God into this mess.

"Hey," I said with too much enthusiasm as I rushed to meet Simone and Skye at the landing. "I was wondering what happened to you guys."

Neither Simone nor Skye said a word; both just glared across the room at Quintin. And he stared right back at them.

The air was so thick with tension that I wasn't sure Simone was going to hear me through the fog, but I talked anyway. "I was thinking we should do another song."

"I thought we were only going to do one," she whispered with her eyes still on Quintin.

I swear it looked like she was about to cry. And if she did, I was gonna kill Q, right here, right now. "Yeah, but you did so well," I said, wanting to reassure her, "that I was thinking we may want to do two tracks."

She shook her head. "I . . . I . . ." she stuttered, as if she was trying to come up with the right thing to say. "I have to go . . . for a study group."

I knew that was a lie, but how could I stop her from leaving? And, anyway, it was probably better that she left. Then Quintin and I could have it out, because there was no way that I was giving up on Simone.

"Okay," I said as Skye stomped past me. For a moment, I thought Simone's sister was going after Quintin. But all she did was grab her purse from the chair. She did pause for a moment, and stare Quintin down, but my frat brother was too arrogant to care.

She swung her purse over her shoulder, just missing Quintin's nose by inches. Then, she marched back across the room, took her sister's hand, and trudged up the stairs. Silently, I followed the two, wondering if I should say something to Simone. But I didn't want to embarrass her any further. I would catch up with her later, take her out to dinner, and tell her to ignore the idiot who fronted as my business partner.

I opened the front door for them and gave Simone a tight hug. "You were fantastic!" I whispered into her ear. "I'll call you later."

Her head was down as she nodded and spun away from me. All Skye did was look at me with a stare that told me that if I didn't take care of my friend, she would. I nodded slightly, and with my eyes told her that I had this whole situation under control.

Usually, I stood and watched Simone pull her car out of the driveway. But not today. I couldn't wait to close the door. I couldn't wait to go back downstairs and have it out with Quintin!

Chapter 17

"Code Red! Code Red!"

That was the special signal out among our friends—whenever there was an emergency, Chyanne, Devin, Skye, or I sent out a Code Red. And that's what Skye had been yelling into her cell from the moment we backed out of Jaylen's driveway. I wasn't sure what had come first, her cries out to our friends or my tears that just wouldn't stop.

She's fat! There was a lot more that Quintin had said, but those two words were the ones that were stuck in my mind. I'd had a lifetime of people saying mean things about my weight, but at least most pretended that they weren't trying to hurt my feelings. No one had ever been so straight in my face the way Quintin was this morning. Sure, I wasn't exactly standing in front of him when he went off about how I would never be a Tru Harmony artist, but he knew I was in the house. He knew I would hear him.

I was beyond grateful when Skye found a parking space right in front of my dorm. It was going to be hard enough hiding my tearstained face without having to walk halfway across campus with my head down. I jumped out of her BMW, and was able to keep my cries inside until we rushed into my room and I fell across my bed. Then, I really let it rip.

"Come on," Skye said as she sat on the edge of the bed and tried to soothe me. "You can't let this guy get to you."

"How can I not let him get to me?" I said in a tone that sounded like my sister was crazy. "Quintin is one of Jaylen's partners. And if he says that he doesn't want me, then I'll never be part of Tru Harmony," I wailed.

"That's not true. Jaylen wants you. And so does Miles—"

"But not Quintin!"

"Quintin is an ass!"

I was so shocked by my sister's declaration that, for a moment, I stopped crying.

"Well, he is," she continued when she saw my expression. She stood up and began to pace the length of my room. "After the way you sang, Quintin should be on his knees thanking God for bringing you into their pitiful company."

Yeah, I thought. *That's what he should have been doing.* But Quintin wasn't anywhere close to talking to the Lord about me, and just thinking about what he was probably saying to Jaylen at this moment had me crying all over again.

For the last three weeks, I'd been so hyped, walking around actually believing that I was going to be a real singer. But it looked like my dreams were ending before they started.

Why did I keep doing this to myself? Why did I keep getting my hopes up so high? My father tried to tell me, but, no, I wouldn't listen. Well, Quintin had done what my father wasn't able to do: Quintin took that dream right out of my heart, grabbed it, tossed it on the floor, and stomped on it. I wasn't about to put myself in a situation like that ever again. The days of dreaming, of believing, were over.

In the middle of my cries, my cell phone rang. I reached for it, thinking it was Chyanne or Devin, but then pulled my hand back when I looked at the screen.

"Who's that?" Skye asked.

I didn't answer her, just switched the phone to vibrate. But even without lifting my head, I knew Skye had figured it out.

"You need to talk to him and get this straightened out."

I did want to talk to Jaylen. Badly. But what was I supposed to say? And what was he going to say? He would try to make me feel good. Probably even tell me not to listen to Quintin. But my decision was made. There was no way I was going to come between two friends. And there was no way I was going to be the reason why the label wasn't successful. I was just going to walk away . . . now!

"So, what?" Skye broke through my thoughts. "You're not going to talk to him?"

I shook my head.

"Why not?"

How could I explain to my strong, beautiful sister that I was so over this drama? How could I tell her that there was no need for me to fight because the fat girl never won? How could I tell her that I wasn't her?

When I didn't say anything, Skye threw her hands up in the air. "This is ridiculous," she shouted, like she was mad at me. "I *know* you're not going to give up."

"Give up what?"

Fresh tears were streaming out of my eyes when I looked up. Chyanne and Devin walked into my room without knocking, like they always did, but today they weren't wearing smiles.

Skye hadn't told them what happened. She didn't have to. When we sent out Code Reds, the only thing we asked was when and where. Knowing my friends, after Skye had told them to meet us at my dorm, Chyanne and Devin had hooked up and then driven here, probably at a hundred miles an hour.

But now that they were here, they wanted to know what was up. Just the thought of repeating what Quintin had said sent me into a new crying frenzy, leaving Skye to fill our friends in.

"Where is he?" Devin demanded to know after Skye finished the story.

"Why?" Chyanne asked with her hands on her hips. "What are you going to do?"

"I'm not gonna do nothin'." Devin waved his hands in

the air. "You think I wanna mess up my fresh manicure?" He leaned back on my bed. "But I got some boys who'll handle this," he said. "Trust."

"Oh, please," Chyanne said. "Your *boys* ain't gonna do a thing." Then, she turned to me. "But what are you gonna do, honey?" She spoke so sweetly, her tone was filled with such sympathy, that I wanted to cry all over again.

"There's nothing I can do. I'm just gonna forget all about Jaylen, Tru Harmony, and the recording contract."

"Why you gonna do that?" the three of them said in unison.

If I weren't so sad, I would've laughed. We really were the best of friends.

"'Cause," I began, getting back to the topic, "it's stupid to keep pursuing this and pursuing this and having my dreams killed all the time."

"That's ridiculous," Skye said. "This is the first time you've ever really pursued being a singer. And just because you came up against an ass doesn't mean that you should give up."

"Tell it!" Devin raised his hand, as if he was part of Skye's amen corner. "Preach, sista! When your daddy retires, you'd better jump into that pulpit, 'cause you sure can preach a good word!"

Chyanne shook her head at Devin, but spoke to me. "Skye's right; you've never been a quitter."

"No, but how am I supposed to fight Quintin? I don't want Jaylen to have to choose between me and his friend."

"You're probably doing the man a favor," Skye said, before she sucked her teeth. "Because Jaylen doesn't need to have a friend like Quintin."

"I agree," Devin piped in. "You're the best thing that ever happened to Jaylen. He's probably over at his house thanking you for showing him what kind of fool he's in business with."

"And that's the key," I said, sitting up on my bed. "They're in business together. Quintin has as much to say about this as Jaylen does."

"That's why you need to march right back over there and curse Quintin the hell out!" Devin shouted.

Skye gave Devin a high five, but Chyanne shook her head.

With a frown, she said, "That's not the way to handle it. You should talk to Jaylen and work it out with him."

Skye said, "That'll work, because I saw the way Jaylen was looking at you; he has your back."

"I don't care what none of you heifers say," Devin jumped in. "Monnie, you need to get back over there and show Quintin what kind of fighter you are. Kick some ass, baby!" he said, as if I were about to go off to war.

"You don't need to do that," Chyanne said.

"She doesn't have to prove a thing to that fool," Skye spoke to Devin.

As my sister and friends went back and forth on how I should handle this, I just lay back. My cell vibrated again, and I glanced at the screen. But my crew didn't even notice, with the way they were arguing back and forth about my life.

My head began to throb as my eyes squeezed out the last of my tears. I'd cried myself right into a headache, and all I wanted to do was lie down and forget about what happened today. But I wouldn't be able to do that; I wouldn't get any rest, any peace, while Skye, Chyanne, and Devin debated what was best for me.

My phone vibrated again, and, this time, three pairs of eyes turned to me.

"Is that Jaylen?" Skye demanded to know.

I nodded.

"Take the call," Chyanne instructed.

That was when I got the idea. "I will call him back later," I said. "I don't want to talk to him in front of you guys."

Skye and Chyanne nodded as if they understood. But not Devin.

"Why can't you talk to him in front of us?" he asked. "Since when do we keep secrets?"

"Come on," Chyanne said, grabbing Devin's elbow. "Let's get out of here."

"Are you sure you're going to be all right?" Skye asked.

"Yeah." I nodded. "This is not the first time I've had to deal with a jackass."

My sister smiled, convinced that I was back to my old self. I was—she just didn't know that I was going *all* the way back, to the old Simone who never dared to dream.

"Okay, we'll get out of here," Skye said as she hugged me.

Chyanne did the same, but when Devin wrapped his arms around me, I could tell that he wasn't as happy as the girls.

"I don't know why we gotta leave now. This was a Code Red, and by definition that means that we should stay the whole night."

"Who told you that?" Chyanne asked, pushing Devin out the door.

I couldn't do anything but smile as I got up off my bed and locked my door. My sister and best friends had my back. They would've done anything to make sure that this thing worked out with me and Tru Harmony. And if I thought it would do any good, I would've turned them loose on Quintin.

But the truth was, my friends were wrong. Quintin was the one who was right. He'd only said aloud what I'd been thinking all along. You had to be really special to be a big girl and make it in this business. This was never going to happen for me, and the sooner I accepted that, the better it would be for everyone.

My cell vibrated again, and this time, I didn't even look at the screen. I just lay back on my bed, and thought about how life was going to be wonderful when I finally started working at Ernst & Young in just a few months. I thought about the money. Almost $50,000 was a lot for a new graduate, and, in this economy, there were millions of people who would do anything to trade places with me.

That was the bright side, and that's what I needed to stay focused on. *The bright side, the bright side*, I said over and over in my head. Then, I closed my eyes, and the bright side faded to black.

Chapter 18

Simone must've had me mixed up with some other dude if she thought she could hide from me. I flipped shut my cell once again. It didn't matter how many calls I had to make. I wasn't about to give up.

"Man, you knew how Q was before we signed up to do this."

Miles's words broke through my thoughts, and I glanced over my shoulder. He was sitting in the chair in the corner where Skye had sat just an hour ago, before hell had broken loose in this basement.

Why did Quintin have to come back home today of all days? Usually, he spent Saturdays out—if he even came home from Friday night. This morning, Quintin had gotten up early, and when he walked out the door, I was sure that Miles and I wouldn't see him until sometime tomorrow after we came home from church. And, even then, my strategy was to not say a word to Quintin until I was ready to present him with a whole package: publicity photos, a marketing plan, and Simone's demo.

But when he'd surprised us and come downstairs, I didn't think it was going to be any kind of problem. He had two ears just like the rest of us. A minute listening to Simone, and I knew he'd be a fan for life.

But he wasn't! And it didn't have a thing to do with her voice. Un-freakin'-believable!

"You know you guys are gonna have to talk about this," Miles said. "We're gonna have to work this out."

"Nothing to talk about," I said. And I meant that.

Obviously, Quintin felt the same way, because after I let Simone and Skye out the house, I came right back down to confront him. But Quintin was already halfway backup the stairs.

"I'm not talking to you about this, Man," he said as he pushed past me.

I pushed him back, making him stumble on the steps. That's when Miles jumped in between us, the way he always had to do.

"Come on, guys," Miles had pleaded as he backed me against the wall. I fought to get out of his grasp, but in the small space of the stairwell, Miles had me kinda trapped.

"Yeah, you better hold him," Quintin said, pointing his finger toward me.

"Yeah, he'd better hold me 'cause you know what's up," I screamed back.

The fact was, the three of us did know what was up. Quintin didn't want any part of me. Not after the way I'd taken him the last time we'd resorted to fisticuffs. Interestingly enough, it was over a woman then too. That time it was about Quintin disrespecting me, trying to talk to a female, Shaniya Green, who I was interested in.

Thinking about that now, I shook my head. It really was a trip that Quintin and I were even friends. The thing was, when we clicked, we clicked. We liked the same things, like video games and the Lakers. We were Trekkies, and the only guys I knew our age who were fans of *Willy Wonka & the Chocolate Factory*. But the biggest kicker was that he was not only frat, he was my line brother. I was number seven and he was number eight. Pledging together, we'd been through hell . . . literally. I had his back and he had mine.

At least, that's how it'd been until today. It looked like the proverbial last straw had broken our relationship. Quintin needed to go his way and I would go mine.

"So I'm gonna call Q," Miles said, even though he had to know that I wasn't trying to hear that. "I'ma tell him to come back here so that we can work this out as boys." When I didn't say anything, Miles added, "As brothers."

I glanced down at my phone, flipped it open, and pressed "2" for the speed dial I had set to Simone. Ignoring Miles, I held the phone to my ear, and heard the four rings again before Simone's cheerful voice mail greeting came on.

Just like all the other times, I clicked off the phone. There was no need to leave a message; Simone knew it was me and she knew why I was calling. Still, I wanted to talk to her, straighten this thing out, let her know that I had her back no matter what. She was in, even if that meant that Quintin had to be out.

"So you're gonna hang while I call Q?"

Why was Miles even talking to me? He'd heard the things Quintin had said. He saw the way Simone had crawled out of this house, thoroughly hurt and totally embarrassed. He had to know how upset I was about that. So, what was there to talk about?

I pushed myself up from the console.

"J, you listening to me?" Miles asked as I walked toward the stairs. "I'm gonna call Q so that we can get together and talk this out," he repeated.

Not even looking at him, I answered, "Do what you have to do."

I meant that. 'Cause I was gonna do what I had to do. The plan was already working out in my head. It was twofold: First, I was gonna do everything in my power to make sure that Tru Harmony still ran smoothly without Quintin. And, after that, I was going to get Simone's first single released.

***

There was only a single light on in the entire house. I took a deep breath as I trotted down the stairs to the foyer, then turned left toward the kitchen, where the overhead light glowed.

I stood at the door stiffly, just staring, then headed straight to the refrigerator. I reached for a bottle of beer, but then grabbed a water instead, since I had to be up for church in just a few hours. Walking back across the room, I banged my bottle down on the glass-top table, resting it next to Quintin's beer. Then, I sat down across from him.

Just like he'd been doing from the moment I'd entered the kitchen, Quintin kept his gaze centered on the window, staring into the middle-of-the-night blackness. There was no way he could see anything, but I could tell that he was deep in thought. Exactly the way I'd been up in my room. Which was why I couldn't sleep, and why I'd heard Quintin come in about a half hour before.

When I didn't hear Quintin come up the stairs, I knew he was down here, probably having a beer. That was when I decided that now was as good a time as any for us to have it out. Maybe in the midnight hour, cooler heads would prevail. Maybe in the dark of the night, we'd be able to talk as brothers who had some sense.

"That was really messed up, man," I began my opening statement. "What you did to Simone . . . that was really messed up."

He took another swig of his beer as if he needed time to think of an answer. Putting his bottle down, he said, "I didn't do anything to her," as if he didn't have any sense at all.

I had to grasp my hands together in what looked like a single fist to stop myself from decking him right there. How could he say that? How could he be so nonchalant about hurting someone's feelings?

I thought about how I had wanted this to be a peaceful discussion, and held back my anger. "You know you wrong," I said as calmly as I could. "You know you hurt that girl and that wasn't necessary."

Finally, he nodded. Finally, he looked at me. "A'ight. Next time you see her, tell her sorry for me."

Lord, grant me the serenity . . . That was the prayer that kept my fist away from his jaw. "What's your problem?" I asked with an edge in my tone.

"Success," he said simply. "I figure if we do this, we might as well do it right."

"I'm with you. That's why I picked Simone. Man, tell me that girl can't sing."

He held up his hands. "She can sing, I'll give you that. But you and I both know that this industry doesn't have a thing to do with singing."

I nodded. "But we agreed we were going to be different. We agreed we were going to be all about the art."

"True dat, but you can't tell me that there isn't a female out there with a voice and the look. There has to be someone. You just haven't searched hard enough."

"I haven't because I found Simone." I paused. "Man, have you *heard* her sing?" I repeated, wanting him to know just how dumb I thought his argument was.

"So what are we gonna do? Ask everyone who buys her single to wear blindfolds?"

Ouch! That hurt. He wasn't even talking about me and my feelings were all the way hurt. "She's not ugly," I defended.

"Not ugly, just big."

"Why you keep trippin' on that?"

"Because in this industry, big is ugly."

"But what about all the big girls who've made it?"

"First of all, there are not many of them, and, secondly, just ask the ones who did make it how hard it was for them."

"But—"

Before I could finish, he held up his hand. "I'll give it to you, Simone can sing, but she needs to stick to gospel 'cause there ain't nothin' but big girls there."

I could not believe he said that. Just like everyone else in her life, Quintin wanted to push her to the other side of soul. What was that about?

Quintin continued, "Look, I've said this before. Coming out of the gate, we've got to be straight. Simone's not the one for us."

I shrugged. "So where does this leave us? 'Cause, man, I'm not gonna budge on this."

He blew out a long, frustrated breath. "What's up? Why it gotta be Simone?"

I shook my head. That was a good question, but not one that I could answer with words. I didn't know exactly *why* it had to be Simone, I just knew that it *had* to be her. I was sure of that. Tru Harmony was going to put Simone on the map, and Simone was going to put Tru Harmony on the map. It was a win-win; I could feel that deep in my bones.

I said, "I wanna win. That's why it's gotta be Simone."

Quintin took a final swig of his beer. "Miles is gonna vote with you," he said as if he knew where this fight was going.

"That's how we set this up." I nodded. "Anytime we didn't agree, we'd take a vote."

"You and Miles don't know what it takes to make this label work."

"Are you kidding me? I'm the one who knows talent. You don't have a musical bone in your body." That was a half joke, meant to lighten the moment. But Quintin didn't crack a smile.

"You're right," he said. "You're the music man, but I'm like Jay-Z, a businessman all the way. I know how to win."

"Well, I guess we have different definitions of what it's gonna take to win. Guess we're not in true harmony after all." I paused. From the moment Quintin had stomped out of the house earlier, I'd been thinking about this. "If you don't think Miles and I are winners, you can always step away. I'll buy you out."

"With what money?" He smirked.

He had no idea what steps I'd already taken. "I called my parents. They're willing to lend it to me."

Quintin's eyes were huge when he turned to me. My frat knew that I never went to my parents for anything, especially not money. But if I had called them for this, then this was a different kind of game.

I said, "They're willing to lend me whatever I need. I'll buy you out, man, 'cause I'm not gonna back down."

Our eyes were stuck in some kind of stare-lock before Quintin turned away. His glance returned to the window, to the darkness of the night. Finally he said, "Here's the deal, if Simone doesn't work, I pick the next ten artists."

I smiled just a little. "The next five."

"Eight."

"Seven," I said, just because I had to have the last word. I wasn't worried about having to pay up. Simone was going to more than work for Tru Harmony.

After a few seconds, he turned back, looked at me, and held up his fist. I bumped my fist against his, sealing the deal. Shaking his head as if he couldn't believe that he'd given in, he pushed back his chair. "So what date are you shooting for, for the release?"

"Can I get back to you on that? Still trying to work out the plan."

He nodded before he turned and walked away, leaving me alone. When I heard Quintin close his bedroom door, I let out a deep breath. Tru Harmony was still intact.

Now, all I had to do was make sure that the singer I'd fought so hard to keep still wanted to work with us. I had to make sure that Simone was still on board. But I had a feeling that as hard as it was to work this out with Quintin, talking to Simone was going to be no easy feat. It was a good thing that tomorrow I'd see her in church, because my prayer was that in the Lord's house, she'd hear God's voice and have to answer His call. And I had no doubt that meant she would sing with Tru Harmony.

Chapter 19

I had never lied to my parents before.

Well, I guess that wasn't completely true. I mean, just like everyone else, I'd told little lies all the time. Like in elementary school, I told my parents that I didn't know how that bubblegum got into my backpack. And in junior high, I always lied about not having homework over the weekend. Then, the big one—in high school, I told my parents that I was going to see a movie called *God's Army*, when the truth was, Devin and I snuck in to see *Romeo Must Die*.

But those were little lies compared to this whopper that I'd just told. Nothing could compare to telling my parents this morning that I was missing church because my stomach was so upset that I was up all night.

At least part of that lie was true. I had been up all night, but it wasn't an upset stomach that kept me awake. It was Quintin's words, and the way they taunted me inside my mind. Plus, it was the way Jaylen kept calling. I could have turned my phone off, but it made me feel just a little bit better to know that Jaylen cared enough to blow up my cell, although his caring wasn't enough. This dream of mine was so over. I just had to get Jaylen to understand that, and he would, once I ducked and dodged him enough to make him give up. My plan was that it would only take a week for Jaylen to get the message. At least, that was my hope. Because I could hide from him easy enough during the week, but next Sunday I'd have to have my butt in church. No way was Reverend Davenport going to allow me to be absent two weeks without a note from a doctor.

The Sunday morning light was peeking through a corner of the blinds at my window, but I wasn't having it. There was no room for any kind of sunshine in my life right now, so I pulled the covers over my head. It wasn't going to be hard to stay in bed and sleep away my depression, since my head throbbed from misery and pain.

The loud knock almost made me sit up, but I just turned my back to the door and rolled closer to the wall. I had no idea who was trying to get at me, but it didn't matter, 'cause all the folks I cared about were in church. But my ignoring the continuous knocking didn't make the person go away, and when I heard the lock on the door jiggle, I sat straight up.

"Hey," my sister said as she peeked around the door.

I sighed a little with relief, but then I bounced back on the bed, sorry that I'd ever given Skye a key. It had seemed like a good idea at the time, because of emergencies and everything. But now that I wanted some peace, I wished that big sis didn't have this kind of access to me.

"How did you know that I was here?" My voice was muffled since I was still tucked under the covers.

"Chyanne told me that you'd told her not to pick you up this morning."

Still hiding beneath the blanket, I said, "I told her that I was going to drive myself," repeating the lie I'd told our best friend.

"You never drive to church, and, after yesterday, I knew that meant you were locked up in here."

Dang! My sister knew me way too well. Chyanne drove me to church just about every Sunday so that I always had an excuse not to go to my parents' house afterward. I guess that strategy was working against me today.

"So why didn't you go to church?" Skye asked.

Even though I couldn't see her, I could feel her standing over me. I didn't respond, hoping that by not saying anything, she would go away. But after a couple of silent seconds, my sister snatched the covers back, exposing me completely.

"Dang! You didn't even take off your clothes!" Skye exclaimed, looking down at the jeans and shirt that I still had on from yesterday. "What's up with that? What's wrong with you?"

How could she ask me that? As if she didn't know.

"I thought you said you weren't going to let that idiot get to you."

"I lied," I said, sitting up in the bed since it was apparent that my sister wasn't going to go away.

"I don't get it. Quintin means nothing to you."

"But Jaylen does. And Quintin is his business partner. I'm not going to mess this up for them."

"Oh, brother." Skye rolled her eyes. "What do I have to say to get you to understand that Jaylen ain't thinking about Quintin?"

"Maybe you can't say anything to her, Skye."

I felt whiplash coming on with the way I snapped my head to the left and stared at Jaylen standing in the doorway. My eyes got big and I couldn't move. I guess Skye felt the same way, because she was standing so still, she could've been a statue.

"What are you doing here?" I didn't mean to whisper, but that's the way my words came out—just barely, because it was hard for me to even breathe.

"I came to check on you," he answered, his voice just as soft as mine. Jaylen nodded his hello at Skye, then moved toward my bed. My heart was beating so hard now that my chest ached as much as my head. "How're you feeling?"

I nodded, because the words wouldn't come out of my mouth. It wasn't just the shock from Jaylen being in my room that had me speechless. It was partly because of the way he looked. When Jaylen turned to shut the door that Skye had left open, I couldn't help but see the way his black tailored pants hugged his butt. And if his shirt could speak, it would be bragging about the muscles in his chest and the way his arms were cut.

Finally, Skye backed away from the bed as if she wanted to make room for Jaylen. I wanted to snatch her back, but it was hard for me to move since I still wasn't breathing.

"Your moms said you were really sick," Jaylen said as he looked at me. His eyes were squinted as he gave me the once-over, like he was a doctor checking for symptoms. For a moment, I could tell that he really thought I was sick. I guess I did look pretty bad from a long night of sleeplessness.

"Not really sick," I said, getting my voice back. "Just a little . . ."

I didn't finish, but Jaylen nodded as if I had. As if he understood what I said *and* what I didn't say. He said, "I'm sorry about what happened yesterday."

I shrugged. "Not your fault."

"Nah, it is. I should've taken care of Quintin before I got you involved, but it's all cool now."

It was my turn to squint. "What are you talking about?"

"Quintin and I talked and he's fine with you being our first artist, so we can just keep moving forward with our plans."

I shook my head. "You're not just saying that, are you?" It wasn't that I didn't believe him . . . well, truth? I really *didn't* believe him. I mean, with the way Quintin had talked, I couldn't see him being fine with anything that had to do with me.

"Nah, I wouldn't lie to you about this."

"It's not that I think you're lying. It's just that . . ." I had to pause, because just thinking about what Quintin had said made all of these sad feelings rise up inside me. "Quintin didn't sound like he would ever change his mind."

"Well, he did. And even if he didn't, Miles and I wanted you, so what Quintin said didn't matter."

Okay, that wasn't exactly a resounding endorsement. It didn't sound like Quintin was on board at all.

"But what Quintin said did matter," I said. "Because he was only telling the truth."

Jaylen frowned as if he didn't understand what I was saying. I said, "Have you ever noticed that I *am* fat?" There! I said it. I had to get that out.

Across the room, I heard my sister groan. I had actually forgotten that Skye was there, but I didn't look at her. My eyes stayed on Jaylen, who shook his head at my words. "Let me tell you what I have noticed about you," he began. "I noticed that you can sing."

I could sing? That was the best he could come up with?

"And I noticed that you're beautiful. Really beautiful, Simone."

My mouth opened wide at that one, because I was shocked and I needed air. I'd had guys say some decent things about me before—that I had a pretty face, that I was nice, that I was special. But beautiful was not a word that many used to describe me.

"Aww." That was Skye again, all up in my business.

"Look, Simone." The way he said my name made me forget all about my sister. "I know you were hurt by what Quintin said yesterday, and I'm so sorry about that. If Quintin were here, he'd apologize too."

Okay, up until that point, Jaylen had me. But Quintin apologizing? That I had a hard time believing.

He said, "I could stand here and argue you down about all the big girls who've made it. But none of them and none of that matters to me, because I'm only thinking about you and your success. Simone, I know how big you're gonna be."

My eyes got really wide at his choice of words, but Jaylen was quick to clean it up.

"I mean . . . you know what I mean, right?"

He looked so sorry, all I could do was smile and nod.

Jaylen said, "Now maybe Quintin's not your biggest fan . . . right now. But since my boy is all about the Benjamins, he'll love you as much as I do very soon."

"Oh!" Skye was all up in this as if she were watching her favorite soap opera. "So see, Simone? Everything's fine," my sister sang.

It may have sounded fine to Skye, but I still wasn't sold. At least, not until Jaylen held out his hand. I just stared at him for a moment before I took it. He pulled me up from the bed. "Simone, you are the best singer I've heard in a long time, and I know that God has great plans for you. The bottom line is that Miles *and* Quintin are behind you, but most of all, I want you."

The way he looked at me and the way he sounded made it seem like Jaylen was no longer talking about my singing. But I wasn't trying to figure it out, because I'd never heard words so sweet.

Then, Jaylen did something even sweeter. He pulled me into his arms and hugged me tightly. He held me as if I were his girlfriend or something. And he didn't seem to even care that Skye was sitting right there. The truth was, I didn't care either.

So I closed my eyes and hugged him back, until I heard my door squeak open. Dang! It seemed that my room had turned into Hartsfield Airport. I hadn't had this many visitors all semester. I wasn't sure if it was Chyanne or Devin. Probably the both of them.

But then the door fully opened and I jumped right out of Jaylen's arms. If my heart was beating hard before, there was not a word for the way it was beating now.

My father stood at the door with the deepest frown on his face. And that was when I started shaking.

***

I had no idea how much time had passed—ten seconds, ten minutes. Actually, it felt like ten hours had gone by before anybody in the room even breathed. My father stepped completely inside the room with my mother trailing behind him.

"We thought you were sick." My father's strong voice boomed against the walls of my tiny dorm room. "Your mother and I wanted to check on you." Then, he turned from me and glared at Jaylen, his eyes moving up, then down, as if he was trying to tell Jaylen just how much disdain he had for him. The way my father looked stopped my heart cold, but I didn't breathe any easier when he turned away. Because now, he was staring at Skye with the same contemptuous scrutiny.

I stood there, just waiting, just knowing that I was next. But my father didn't come back to me. Instead, he took giant steps that took him right up to Jaylen.

Please, Lord, I prayed inside. I stopped my prayer after those two words, because I wasn't sure what I was asking God. But I figured that since He knew my heart, He'd figure it out.

My dad was all up in Jaylen's face when he asked, "What are you doing here?"

"I . . . I . . . I . . ."

Oh, Lord. Jaylen was as scared as I was. I turned to Skye, and inside I yelled out to her. I'd read that sisters who were close were supposed to be able to read each other's thoughts. I needed her to know that I needed her to do something, to jump in right in and save me and Jaylen.

But Skye didn't move. Not that she looked scared. She didn't, as she sat with her arms folded and a deep frown on her face. But it didn't look like she was about to get involved in this, either. If only Chyanne were here, she'd jump in the middle. She'd save everything.

It took him a couple of seconds, but finally, Jaylen got it together. "I . . . just came to check on Simone. Mrs. Davenport"—he paused, and looked at my mother as if he expected her to come to his side—"told me Simone wasn't feeling well, and I wanted to make sure that she was all right."

"There's no reason for you to be here," my father said as if Jaylen was an intruder. "Taking care of my daughter is my job. You're nothing more than a piano player."

"Daddy!" I meant to scream out that word, but it only came out as a whisper.

I don't think it would've mattered how loudly I spoke, because it didn't seem like my father was trying to hear anything that anyone had to say. He was already on Skye.

"And I know why you're here," my father started.

Skye raised one eyebrow as if she wanted him to know that she wasn't scared, and she was ready for any kind of fight.

My father said, "You just want to start trouble. Why don't you stay away and leave your sister alone? She's doing fine without you."

I started praying again. This time my appeal to God was for Him to keep Skye's mouth shut, because I knew if she said a word, it wasn't going to be pretty. But before God could answer me, Skye proved that I was right.

"This is the first time that you set eyes on me in two years and this is what you have to say?" she asked all boldly. Skye shook her head. "I'm not even going to let you come at me like that."

My father's eyes got wide. "I am your father, young lady!"

"And that's my point. Because no father should talk to his daughter this way." She made a sound that was something like a chuckle, even though I didn't think she was laughing. "But what would I expect from you? Of course you would talk this way after the way you've treated me!"

There was nothing I could do now to save the situation except maybe sit down in the middle of the floor and cry. I couldn't believe this was playing out right in front of Jaylen. I wanted to push him out of the room and ask him to pretend that he'd never been in the middle of this family drama.

But then, our mother stepped in, right between Skye and my father, as if she felt like she had to protect Skye. Or maybe with the way Skye was trembling with anger, my mother thought that the reverend was the one who needed protection.

She said, "Skye, your father has always wanted what was best for you."

Skye said, "Daddy doesn't want what's best for me or Simone." She spoke as if he weren't standing right there. "He just wants what's best for him. He just wants to portray himself as the perfect *Reverend Davenport*," she said as if his name disgusted her, "with the perfect children who do exactly what he wants them to do."

I could only think of one thing to stop all of this, and that was to pretend that it wasn't happening. I could just act like my father hadn't walked into my room and caught me in a lie. Just act like my mom and dad had just walked in. That's exactly what I did. I took the few steps to my father, figuring that if I hugged him, I could make most of these bad feelings go away. "Thanks for coming, Daddy," I said. But when I hugged him, he didn't exactly hug me back. "I was sick earlier, but I'm glad you came by. Just like I'm glad that Skye came, and Jaylen too."

It was like when I said his name that reminded my father that Jaylen was there.

"You need to leave," he said in a not-so-nice tone. "And just stay away from her. I know you've probably been filling her head with silly dreams."

I couldn't believe my father was acting like this. But before I could defend Jaylen, he defended himself.

"They're not silly dreams," Jaylen said. "I have a record label. And I have a studio. My partners and I are signing Simone to a recording contract."

"No!" my father said as if he were in charge of me. "She's

going to graduate and work for one of the biggest firms in the country. Do you know how much they're willing to pay her?"

I stood there, astonished, trying to find the right words to stop this nightmare that was playing out in front of me.

But Jaylen took over. "Yeah, I know all of that, Reverend Davenport. Because Simone and I talked about everything so that we wouldn't be making this decision lightly. But this is her dream, and—"

"Oh, please!" my father said, interrupting Jaylen. "Dreams don't pay the bills." He paused. "So, you talked about this, huh? Then how much are you willing to pay her? How much are you willing to give her to make sure that she can support herself? Because if she does this then . . ."

He stopped short of telling all of us that I was going to suffer the same fate as my sister; I was going to be thrown out of his life.

Now, what I wanted to do was sit in the middle of the floor and cry. But I stood there, - like I was a big girl. Like I wasn't at all affected by the things my father was saying.

Jaylen said, "Simone and I talked about the money, too. Of course, there won't be any money at first . . ."

My father laughed, though we could all tell that he didn't find anything funny. "Of course there won't be any money," he said, repeating Jaylen's words. His face was once again so serious when he looked directly at me. "This is a pipedream," he said.

"Even if it is, it's her dream," Skye piped in.

Oh, God! Could this get any worse?

His eyes became thin slits when he said to Skye, "Get out of here!" Before I could say anything, he demanded the same of Jaylen. "Both of you, get out of here."

"No!" I couldn't believe that shocking word came from me. And from the way everyone looked at me, especially my father, I knew no one else could believe it either. So since I started, I decided to finish. "Dad, you can't throw people out of my room." Before he could say it, I did. "I know you pay all of the bills, but even though I love and respect you, you can't just come in here . . ."

It was the way he looked at me that made me stop. All of the mad that was on his face went away, and all that was left was hurt. My father looked at me as if I were slipping away, and I wanted to hug him again. But I just stood where I was.

"I'm just trying to protect you," he said, a combination of love and pleading in his tone. "You don't know what it's like, Simone. It would be such a mistake."

"But it would be my mistake," I tried to explain. "You've got to let me make my own mistakes."

He shook his head so hard, I thought he might hurt himself. "No."

"Daddy, I've tried and tried to make this go away, but it won't. Singing is just a part of me, and I really want to give this a try."

"No," he said again.

"I have to."

"No, you can't."

"I have to," I repeated, wanting him to really hear me.

"I said you can't! Don't you understand?"

I frowned. "Understand what?"

"Understand that it's just a stupid dream. And that same stupid dream killed my father!"

It was so quiet, so still, until my mother took slow steps toward my father. Then, with her hand gently on his shoulder, she guided him across the room toward the only chair, where Skye was sitting. My sister, who seemed to be in the same trance I was, jumped up, making room for the man she'd just about cussed out a minute ago. But now, my sister's eyes were wide like mine, full of questions. And like me, she stayed quiet and just stared.

When my father sat down, he bent forward and rested his

elbows on his legs. "I can't let you do this." Even though he was speaking to the floor, I knew his words were meant for me. "It's a curse that's followed our family."

Okay, I had a feeling that my father's words were supposed to scare me. And maybe they would have if I weren't so confused. We had a rich history of pastors in our family, so how could we be cursed?

"I wanted to be a singer all my life," my father said so softly that I wanted to get closer to really hear him. But like everyone else in my dorm room, I stayed right in place.

He continued, "When I was a little boy, I was in awe of all those Motown greats—James Brown, Marvin Gaye, Smokey Robinson." He shook his head. "I wanted to be just like them."

My dad had never told me that he wanted to sing, but I wasn't surprised. From the time I was a little girl, I loved my father's voice. He could sing for real; even when he talked, it sounded like a song.

"But my parents had different plans for me. I was supposed to follow my father into the ministry." For the first time, he looked up, straight at Skye. "I was the firstborn," he said, keeping his eyes on Skye. "And that was our family's tradition. For generations, the firstborn Davenports became pastors."

Whoa! In just a few words, my father had answered a lifetime of questions for me. That's why he wanted Skye to become a minister, even though she never had one iota of interest.

Moving nothing but my eyes, I looked at Skye. I couldn't see all of her face because of the way she was turned, but from what I could see, she was as affected by our father's words as I was.

He said, "But even though I knew what my father wanted for me, I didn't care. I wanted to do my own thing. I was grown and had to be my own person. I had to follow my own dreams."

His words were exactly the ones that Skye had said to him a couple of years ago, and were the ones I was now trying to get him to understand.

Turning to me, he said, "My father told me not to do it," he said, once again turning his glance down as if he couldn't face us as he talked. "But I went out there anyway. Even when my mother called me every day to tell me that I was breaking my father's heart, I didn't care. I took the little bit of money I had, moved to Detroit, and waited to become the next great thing to be discovered by Motown.

"And then, one day I called home. I needed some money, and my father told me he wasn't going to give me a thing. I should've just hung up," he said, shaking his head. "But I was twenty-two years old, dead set on proving that I was a man." He took a deep breath as he glanced up again and looked straight at Skye. "So I told my father exactly what I thought of him treating me, his own child, that way."

Wow! My dad's words were just like the ones Skye had said to him. I wasn't sure where my father was going with this, but when I glanced at Skye, she seemed to know more than I did. Her eyes were filled with water; her tears weren't far away.

"That's what I told my father. Those were my last words to him." My heart started beating faster. He finished with, "I hung up the phone thinking that I'd given him a good piece of my mind. Ten minutes later, he was dead from a heart attack."

My father sobbed. Or maybe he didn't. Maybe it was my mother who released that sad cry. Or maybe it was my sister, with the tears now rolling down her face.

Or maybe it was me. Because I was having a hard, hard time standing up and listening to the pain in my dad's voice.

"I killed my father!" This time, I was sure. It was my father who'd sobbed.

"No, baby. No!"

This was a scene that I'd never seen. My mother knelt next to my father, trying to soothe him.

"It was his heart, baby," my mother said with such sincerity that I wondered how many times she'd had to say those words to my dad. Were these demons that he lived with every day?

"It wasn't you," she kept repeating.

Suddenly my dad looked up, and, this time, his glance zeroed in on me. As I stood stiffly, he sniffed back tears and stared right in my face.

There was a war waging inside of me. One side wanted to rush to my father and promise that I would never sing again. Tell him that I would be a good accountant. That I would never speak badly to him. That I would never kill him.

But as much as I wanted to do that, I stayed strangely still. Because the warrior in me was stronger. I didn't speak a word, but I knew that my father could see the real me. I knew that all he had to do was look through the windows that led to my soul. And there, I knew he would see that I was just like him. He would see that not only had he gifted me with his voice, he'd passed on his dreams. Now, I had to do this, because I had a real chance. I had to do this . . . for myself and for him.

My father took unsteady steps toward me. I held my breath, praying that I would stand for what I truly believed. "You have to do this, don't you?"

I nodded, because there was no way that I could speak.

"I don't like it."

I nodded again.

Now, he nodded, too. And after a few moments said, "Do what you have to do."

Then, without a kiss or good-bye, my father turned and walked right out of my room. Just a second later, my mother hugged me and Skye before she rushed to follow him.

I stayed still in the middle of the silence and the sadness that my father had left behind. Skye shook as she sat on the edge of my bed, but though I wanted to console her and have her console me, I didn't move. I just stayed where I was, remembering each of my father's words. Even in the memory, I could still feel his pain. And it hurt . . . really hurt.

Until I felt his arms. I felt him before I remembered that he'd been there. Jaylen. He didn't say a word as he pulled me into his arms. He said nothing, just held me close.

It wasn't long before I started to cry.

Epilogue

I could not believe they had me in this red dress!

As I twisted in front of the mirror, I checked out my butt. It was still there, for the whole world to see, but it just wasn't as big as it was before. Turning to the front, I had to smile. I was far from being a little girl, but I wasn't as big as I used to be. The Tru Harmony Image Department had worked it. The Tru Harmony Image Department—that made me giggle.

The Image Department was nothing more than Skye, Chyanne, and Devin, who were unofficial, unpaid employees of Tru Harmony. Chyanne was my nutritionist; she kept me focused on being healthy and eating right. For the last six months, Chyanne had me writing down every single thing I ate. At first, that seemed silly, until I noticed that I had to write down a lot. I embarrassed myself into writing less. And less meant fewer calories. And those fewer calories helped me to start losing a little bit of weight.

Then, there was my sister. Skye was my stylist. And the designs she made for me . . . wow! My sister could make me look good in anything, and she came up with outfits that were totally flattering to my figure. But Skye didn't stop there; she taught me how to really shine when I walked into a room.

"It's not just about what you wear, it's about how you wear it," Skye told me.

And Skye taught me how to wear it. She taught me how to strut, not walk. How to pose and not just stand. She taught me how to work it.

Lastly, there was Devin, my personal trainer. He may have acted like a fool twenty-three hours a day, but that one hour when he had me in the gym four times a week, Devin was straight-up as serious as a heart attack! And, sometimes, I felt like I was about to have one, with the way he had me running on the treadmill until enough sweat poured off me to fill a pool, and lifting weights until I was sure that my arms would break. Devin worked me as if I were preparing for the Olympics. But even though I screamed and cursed him out whenever we were in the gym, now, as I looked at myself, all I could do was thank him. Today, I was wearing a sleeveless dress that was cinched at my waist, and, because I had a little shape to my arms and had been doing a million sit-ups, I wasn't self, conscious at all. I was still a long way from looking model-perfect like my girls, Skye and Chyanne, but I was looking like a pretty good me.

Although I had to give it to my crew, the biggest change in me came because of Jaylen. He believed in me so much that I had to start believing in myself. While my girls and Devin had changed me on the outside, Jaylen had worked on the inside.

"Jaylen."

Just whispering his name made me feel warm all over. Since April, when my father had the big blowup in my room in front of everyone, Jaylen hadn't left my side, or at least it felt that way. After my graduation, he worked with me for hours on music, stage presence, how to have a memorable show; the whole aspect of an artist. He did everything he could to get me ready for this day.

Today. My showcase.

I couldn't believe it. I was a singer for real. And today the world was going to know it too.

I'd already had lots of press. Jaylen had articles written about me in all the media that mattered, and he even had me on the red carpet for a couple of minor events.

But today was the day that the world was going to find out all about me—Simone! According to Jaylen, I was going to be a one-name wonder.

I heard the giggles in the hall before the loud knock. But I didn't even get the chance to say come in, when the door opened and my crew busted into my dressing room.

"Hey," Skye, Chyanne, and Devin said in unison.

"Hey." I grinned back.

"These are for you," Devin said, handing me a bunch of flowers that were so heavy I could feel the biceps that Devin had helped me build flex a little. "They're from all of us."

"To wish you well," Chyanne said.

"Thanks."

"I'm so proud of you, sis."

I grinned back at my crew. I'd come a long way with them; none of this would have happened if they hadn't been with me all the way. Especially after what happened with my father. They encouraged me to move forward, especially Chyanne.

"You've got to do what your father didn't have the courage to do," Chyanne had pushed. "I have a feeling that if you do this, it will bring your whole family together."

That had been my prayer, even though so far, that hadn't happened.

"So," Devin said as he bounced back on the sofa, looking like he was about to get comfortable and stay for awhile. "You scared? 'Cause you know there are going to be a lot of people watching you up on that stage.

"Devin!" Chyanne yelled. "Are you *trying* to scare her?"

"It's okay," I said, placing the bouquet on the dressing table. "And to answer your question, no, I'm not scared." I faced my sister and friends like there weren't a million butterflies making their home inside of me. "This is what I've been waiting for all my life."

"And you're gonna be great!" Skye said in just that way that always let me know that she believed in me.

There was another knock on my door, and, this time, whoever was on the other side didn't come barging in. I said to
my crew, "See, this is how you're supposed to do it. You're
supposed to wait for someone to invite you in."

Three pairs of eyes looked at me as if they had no idea what
I was talking about. I shook my head as I opened the door,
and all thoughts of my friends went out the window. How
could I think of anything or anyone else when Jaylen was in
front of me?

"Hey, beautiful."

When Jaylen first started calling me that, I always wanted
to look over my shoulder to see if he was talking to someone
else. I was trying to get used to it, even though it was still
strange to hear someone call me that dozens of times in a day.

He kissed my cheek before he turned to my friends. As they
all greeted one another, I let my thoughts wander back over
the last months. Jaylen and I had spent hours together every
day, perfecting my sound, my look, my image. But the best
hours were the ones we spent just talking, both dreaming out
loud about our future. I thanked him every day for making
my dreams come true. He told me that his would have never
happened if it weren't for me.

But what I remembered most out of all the times we spent
together was the first time that we kissed. I inhaled deeply,
and remembered that day when we were leaning over the console in the studio, and our lips just kinda met, at first. And
then, he pulled me into his arms. And then . . .

"Simone!"

"Huh?" I said, dragging myself away from those delicious
memories.

"Where did you go?" Chyanne asked.

"Nowhere."

"Are you all right?" Skye asked, concern in her voice. "You
look kind of . . ."

I waved my hands. "No, no. I'm fine. I was just thinking." I stopped and looked at Jaylen. "Just thinking about everything."

"Uh-huh!" Devin smirked in a way that made me think he knew exactly what I had been thinking about.

"Okay, guys," Jaylen began, "it's time for you to get out of here."

"Really?" Skye said, and began to wave at her face as if she was trying to keep the tears away. "It's time for the show?"

Jaylen nodded. "She's needs some time to herself. To get into her head and get mentally ready."

"Well, we'll go," Chyanne said, "but first we have to pray."

She reached for my hand and Jaylen's, and then Skye and Devin closed the circle. As we bowed our heads and Jaylen began to ask God to bless this showcase, I felt such a mixture of excitement and sadness. The excitement was about what the next hour would bring, but my sadness was about this moment, and how this prayer should have been given by my father.

Though he no longer said anything negative about my singing, he didn't exactly support it, either. We just never talked about it in our conversations. Not even when I decided to decline the position with Ernst & Young and pursue this full time. I wanted to put my heart and soul into this, the way Jaylen was doing. And though that was a bold move, and though I didn't have a lot of money to back it up, and though I had to move in with Skye until I had some dollars coming through, my father hadn't said a single word to me about it.

I knew my dad knew about all I'd done. He even knew about this showcase. I still told my mom everything and I know she didn't keep anything from him. But there was no chance that he would come, and that meant my mother would stay away too.

"Amen!" everyone said at the end of the prayer.

When I looked up, Devin was staring at Jaylen with glazed eyes as if he was mesmerized. As Skye and Chyanne grabbed their purses from the sofa, I socked Devin in the arm.

"Ow! Why'd you do that?"

"Stop looking at Jaylen that way," I hissed.

"Why? You think you're the only one who wants a good lookin' man who can pray?" He licked his lips like Jaylen was a piece of meat.

"I'm warning you," I said with a grin on my face, but I wasn't playing. Even though Jaylen and I weren't officially boyfriend and girlfriend, we were headed that way for sure, and I needed Devin and everyone else to know that.

"Whatever!" Devin waved his hands, but he didn't take his eyes off of Jaylen.

As Skye and Chyanne hugged me, I didn't take my eyes off of Jaylen either. He leaned against the dressing table, with his arms folded, as he waited for me to finish up with my crew.

Finally, I got the three of them out of the room and turned to Jaylen. He took slow steps toward me, and, when he stopped inches in front of my face, I thought I was going to stop breathing.

"So, are you ready for this?"

I nodded.

"Are you scared?"

"A little," I said, telling him the truth. That's just the way it was between me and Jaylen.

"That's a good thing."

"Really? So the butterflies," I pressed my hand against my stomach, "that won't leave me alone are good."

"Yup. I think it's God's way of keeping you on your toes."

That was a good way to look at it. If I just thought about that fluttering inside of me as God, I couldn't possibly feel bad. Or nervous.

"Well," Jaylen began as he pulled me into his arms. "I'm going to leave you alone for a few minutes."

"Why? I like that you're here."

"I like being here too," he said, then kissed the tip of my nose. And I melted. Right there. He continued, "But you need some personal time alone to get inside your head before you get on that stage."

"I'd rather have you with me until I walk on that stage."

He shook his head. "Soon, you'll be pushing me out the door so that you can get mentally ready."

I couldn't ever imagine a time when I would want to push Jaylen away. But I wasn't going to argue about this. Every single thing that Jaylen had told me was the truth. So I was going to trust him about this, too.

He leaned away from me and looked into my eyes. "I'm so proud of you."

I was mesmerized with the way he captured me with his glance. But it was when he brought his lips to mine so gently, that I was truly gone.

We stayed in that kiss forever, but when he pulled away, it felt like it was too short.

"You're gonna be wonderful," he said, before he strolled out of the room.

When he closed the door, all I could do was sigh. Jaylen always made me do that. Not only because he had made me believe in myself, but he'd taken my heart into his. For the first time in my life, I was in love.

And I was going to be a star.

It was exactly the way I imagined.

The way my heart was beating as the showcase director led me to the stage. The way I stood behind the dark curtain. The way I could hear the excitement of the crowd.

I was trembling from the bottom of my toes to the depth of my soul. But even though I couldn't stop shaking, I couldn't say that I was scared. It was joy bubbling inside of me; this is what I'd waited for my entire life.

I was ready.

"Ladies and gentlemen . . . Simone!"

I stepped on stage, stood there, and I kept my eyes down for a couple of seconds—the dramatic effect that Jaylen had suggested. Then, I looked up; the lights were dimmed, but while I couldn't really see faces, I could tell that the club was filled to capacity.

I closed my eyes and opened my mouth. And when that first note floated out of me, the trembling stopped. I held on to that mic and sang the song that Jaylen and I had decided was going to be the first single.

Every note that I sang came from a place deep inside where I'd kept all my dreams, and, now, it was all coming out of me.

My dream had turned into my life.

I was blessed.

I held the last note as long as I could; not that I was trying to impress anyone—I wasn't. I just wanted to stay in this moment and never let go. But since I needed air, I had to stop.

Hardly a second passed between the time I opened my eyes and the ovation began. There were only a few tables in the club, so just about everyone was standing. But even those in the few chairs stood with the rest and applauded as if I was really a star.

I shivered, though it felt as if it was eighty-five degrees on the stage. I guess my body didn't even know what to do.

As I bowed for the first time, I looked into the audience and my eyes opened real wide. In the front row, in the chairs that had been reserved for the VIPs, there was my mother.

And my father.

Standing and applauding with everyone else.

My parents were really here! All I wanted to do was run off the stage and hug them, especially my father. I knew how hard this had to be for him—my dream, that had once been his dream. His dream, that had turned into a nightmare.

But as he stood and clapped and grinned, I could see his pride. The same look was in his eyes as when he'd talked to me about going to college, as when I'd received the job offer from Ernst & Young. It looked like my father's fears were gone, or at least pushed deep down inside. It seemed like my prayers had come true, that my father could see that God had set this all up for me.

I raised my microphone. "Thank you, Atlanta!" I yelled out the words that I'd been dreaming about, the words that I'd practiced as much as I practiced the song.

Behind the curtains, Jaylen was waiting, his smile so wide and his arms open. It didn't even take me two seconds to get to him and hug him back.

"I did it, Jaylen," I said. "I did it!" I repeated over and over.

"Yeah, you did, beautiful. You nailed it."

I was still holding on to Jaylen when I felt a tap on my shoulder. I turned around and then cried as I fell into my father's arms.

Smoke & Mirrors

A Novella
By Trista Russell

"Is there anything else I can do for you two?" the loud-mouthed bartender asked for the third time since bringing the bill.

"No, thank you." I smiled at him. "I'm done." I looked at the check and wondered how long Jason was planning to let it sit there; he was acting as if we brought it with us. "Are you having another drink?" I hinted at him.

"Nah, I'm good, I'm ready." He slurped the last milliliter of Hennessy through a straw and promptly informed me, "We can cut out of here whenever you pay."

"Excuse me?" I pretended that the music streaming in was too loud. "What did you say?" I leaned toward him.

He spoke louder. "I said just pay and we can go." He looked around like something was stinking. "'Cause I don't like the music in here anyway."

"Wow," I said in shock. I would have paid a hundred dollars for a picture of my face at that very moment. "So, are we splitting the tab in half?" I asked for double confirmation.

"Nah." He shrugged his shoulders, and then said in a voice like I should have known, "I'm broke."

Wait . . . rewind! What? After two months of him straddling the line of professional flirtation and sexual harassment, I agree to go out with him, and he tells me that he has no money? "Are you kidding?" I asked.

"Nah, I won't have money until Friday." He patted his pocket. "You got me, right?"

Got you? "But you asked me out, Jason."

"No." He shook his head. "I told you that I wanted to kick it with you, away from Blare and work stuff."

"Right," I agreed, "you say that every day."

"Right, but today, you said yes," he said, and then clarified, "and then you suggested that we have drinks this evening."

"And you said okay . . ." I shook my head and put my hands up. "Just forget it." I grabbed my purse, snatched my wallet, and pulled my debit card out so fast that the numbers might have come off.

"Garcelle, I told you that I didn't have any money." He lowered his voice so that the people in the lounge wouldn't know that he had insufficient funds. "Remember when I said that I just wanted to sit and talk to you, and get to know you? You were the one who said, 'let's do it over cocktails,' and I clearly said, 'only if you got me.'"

"Well, I thought you meant 'got you' as in giving you a ride." I was trying not to overreact. "It's not a problem, Jason, but, so you know, the next three times are on you."

"No doubt," he said, but quickly amended his answer. "But I will tell you that after child support takes its cut, things get a little tight." He smiled. "But if I have it, I got you."

Blah! Blah! Freakin' blah. I had heard it all before. "We don't have to hang out if it's too much for you." I had to bite my bottom lip so I wouldn't rip him a new one for ballin' out of control on my tab with not one, not two, but three drinks of Hennessy on the rocks.

Jason was twenty-seven years old, extremely handsome, charming, flirtatious, and funny. We worked for Blare Corporation, so I pretty much knew how much he was making, but I didn't expect to buy my own drinks and definitely not his. He was quite a character and the big flirt in the office. In a bout I lost to stupidity, I threw caution to the wind and here we were. It was Friday and I was tired of being lonely, so here I was with a man seven years my junior. Although he closely resembled Ray J, he was an ex-gangbanger with no funds, no ride, a disconnected cell phone, a kid, and God knows what else.

We left the bar and parked a half block away from his bus stop. He continuously apologized for not having money. He felt the need to explain his child support situation, rent, and how his car was repossessed. I felt bad for him, but didn't pity him. I couldn't. My dad used to recite this quote all the time: "For a man to achieve all that is demanded of him, he must regard himself as greater than he is." Jason was a man, and just needed to step up his manly duties and make it work.

It wasn't long before the conversation slithered its way into how he thought my glossy lips were begging to be sucked on. When he moved in close to me, I thought about pulling back, but visions of the seventy-six dollars flashed in my head, and I figured I'd better get something out of the deal. I leaned in toward him, and, when our lips touched, I found that he matched my rhythm, suction, tease, and nibble perfectly. He didn't feel new, and it was like he remembered me. We kissed like high school sweethearts at a ten-year reunion. The passion that spewed from us could only be holstered by him uttering the words, "Damn, I'm hard."

This is where the record screeched to a halt resembling the sound of a frightened cat. "What?" I couldn't believe that he didn't keep that to himself. "You're hard?"

"I'm throbbing, so we better stop." He shifted uncomfortably in the passenger's seat, and pulled away from me. "Damn."

"I'm sorry," I said. "I shouldn't be kissing you anyway." I wiped my lips. "This whole working together thing is a recipe for drama. I don't want to stir up any bad blood with you."

"There is a lot of blood, but none of it is bad." He looked in the direction of his zipper and struggled to gather his thoughts. "You wanna see it?"

Men send dick pictures via text message like they're handing out Halloween candy, so at this point, nothing surprised me. "Sure, if you feel that you have to show it."

"Let me get him for you." He stuck his hand in his pants,

shuffled things around a bit, and then unleashed a beast that did catch me by surprise. Jason wasn't tall, maybe five eleven, and skinny with no real muscles, so seeing him pull out a very thick, can't-really-close-my-fingers-around-it, ten-inch dick was completely amazing to me. I spent the next ten minutes biting my lip and talking myself out of touching it as he stroked it and moaned. "Oh, shit, there's my bus." He quickly packed his dick back into his pants, kissed me on the cheek, and sprinted from my car to the bus stop, screaming out, "See you tomorrow!" as he ran.

On my way south on Lake Shore Drive, I thought of the situation at the bar and laughed aloud. This off-the-wall mess only happens to me, Garcelle Monroe. I always joked about writing a book about the things that happened to me. "How could you hound someone for a date and then not have the money to take them out?" I giggled. I couldn't even call Stacy to tell her about this, but I knew she would ask me why I didn't just leave that ass sitting there. Thank God my mother taught me right. When a man asks you out, always have enough money with you to pay for what you ordered, just in case, but she said nothing about covering his cost too.

"Oh, this is one for the record books." I laughed all the way home. Well, at least *until* I was two blocks from my Hyde Park apartment. I started questioning Jason's real motive. Did he assume that I, a woman carrying a few extra pounds, needed to be graced with a sighting of his dick because I couldn't get one? And was his intention to have me buy his drinks all along? "If his broke ass had a connected phone, I would be making his ears bleed right now, because why was he asking me out all this time knowing he had no money?"

On Monday morning, I did what I needed to do around the building early, so that by the time Jason arrived at noon, I would be buried with work in my office with the door closed. I didn't want to see him or be forced to say hello; I just wanted to forget that the night ever happened. I snuck out for lunch, and went to pick up my dry cleaning, when I caught a glimpse of my reflection in the store's front window. "Wow!" I had forgotten to hold my stomach in. "Oh, God," I gasped. My figure had gone to hell.

I was five foot seven and used to be 160 pounds just three years ago. I had hot dates several times a week, was admired all day long, was fallen in love with countless times, was engaged twice . . . Any man I desired I could have licking my snowy four-inch Chicago boot heel in less than a week, but that was three years ago. Now, at 220 pounds, things just weren't what they used to be. Don't get me wrong, I could still have a man any day of the week; but it just wasn't the same.

A woman with meat on her bones isn't on every man's to-do list, and I can respect that, because a big guy was never on mine. However, men automatically assumed that I was married or had kids. I would have liked men to take one look at me and say, "I'd fuck the shit out of her." Not, "I bet she can cook her ass off." I want, men to fantasize about sweating my perm out, instead of assuming that doing it in the missionary position was all that I was capable of. With the slightest of eye contact, I want, men to know that I could ride that dick as though I was raised on a ranch in Texas.

Living in Chicago, home of deep-dish pizza, Polish sausages, and Harold's Chicken didn't help my situation, but the real problem was my sister's sudden death. A stray bullet struck Danielle when she left a hair-braiding salon one summer night three years ago. She was my best friend, partner in crime, voice of reason . . . She was irreplaceable to me. But because my parents and other siblings were so overwhelmed with grief, I had to be the pillar of strength for our family. It was my shoulder that everyone cried on, so I couldn't cry with them. I cried alone, and found solace in food bite by bite. Now, here I was, the heaviest I had been in my entire life, and I didn't really know how to feel. Don't get me wrong, I loved myself and there were days where my shit didn't stick. My personality was attractive, my sense of humor was always on point, and my intelligence was above average. But I felt like I was not packaged in the right box now. My family and friends were pressing me to create a Facebook account, but the last thing I wanted was for anyone who knew me from my dime piece days to see pictures of me at my current weight.

As soon as I got back from lunch, Carol, who didn't need to put another piece of food in her mouth for at least six months, walked over and announced, "Girl, they have Harold's Chicken in the lunchroom, so you better go grab some."

"Nah, I think I'll pass on that one," I said, looking at Carol's shape and fighting the urge to tell her that she didn't need it either. When I looked at her, I secretly wondered if I was that big and just didn't realize it. Or if I wasn't, I would shamefully pray that God would take away my taste buds if I was ever on the path to being that large. "I can't eat that fried stuff so much anymore," I said, thinking back to the store window.

"It's free chicken, Garcelle!" she said, not used to me turning down food or free anything. "Get in there before those interns do," she joked. "You know their li'l broke asses eat like termites."

I laughed. "Girl, I think I need to start dieting."

"Baby, bye!" She rolled her eyes. "As long as you have a pretty face and a nice personality, you are all good," Carol said. She was married with three kids, so maybe she was right. She had to be about 350 pounds, but she always seemed very confident and never down on herself; I admired that about her. "Girl, please, there's nothing wrong with you." She looked me up and down. "My husband better hope I never make it down to your size, 'cause what?" She whispered, "I'm fucking everything in sight."

"Oh . . ." I was astonished. "Carol, you're a mess."

"Just keeping it real." She smiled. "G, girl, I think the Lord put this weight on me to keep me from being a complete slut."

"What?" I laughed. "Girl, be quiet and get on this diet with me. We can do it together."

"What diet?" she huffed, and acted less than enthused.

"This diet will get you fine and keep you faithful," I played with her.

"Maybe I don't want to be faithful," she said, and then rushed me. "C'mon, tell me about the diet."

"Well, the major part of it is no meat, pop, bread, and other things for about two weeks, and—"

"Wait! No meat?" she interrupted. "Did you say no meat?"

"Yes," I replied guardedly.

"Oh, no." She shook her head from side to side, and her neck fat waved like a flag on a windy day. "No can do. I will die without meat."

"You won't die." I laughed at her. "It's only for two weeks."

"Nah." She waved the flag again.

"Okay." I tried to reason with her. "How about for a week then?"

"For a week?" Carol thought for a moment. "No meat? I don't think I can do that, Garcelle."

"Well, how about no fried food for two weeks then?" I negotiated.

I could tell by the look on her face she wasn't going to do it. "But, you know—"

"Never mind, Carol." I gave up. I knew she would find a way out of anything that didn't lead her straight to the door of a Harold's Chicken Shack.

My office line rang and I sat down to answer it. "This is Garcelle." Carol and I waved good-bye.

"Good afternoon, Garcelle!" The voice on the other line spoke and I nearly passed out right then and there.

"Good afternoon, Cortez," I replied.

With a smile in his tone, he asked, "How's it going?"

"It's going well," I responded. "How are you?"

"I'm fine," he growled. "How's the weather in Chicago?"

"It's January, so let's just say that your Jacksonville weather is sure to be better." I sighed. "It's seventeen here."

"Ouch!" He laughed. "I tried to overnight some sun to you, but the box was too big; FedEx wouldn't ship it."

"Is that right?" I blushed, and giddily poked a pen into the letter "A" on my keyboard repeatedly for no good reason. "Well, all I need is a chunk big enough to shine over my condo, not the entire state."

"Okay," Cortez said. "I'll get that out to you before the end of business today."

Cortez Franklin was an executive who worked from our home office in Jacksonville, Florida. Since being promoted into my new position four months ago, he and I had to talk at least once a week, and I relished each conversation. His seductive baritone voice could make any woman start stepping out of her panties at hello. He was also polite, friendly, and professional, but, every once in a while, his wording would be a tad suggestive.

For the next ten minutes, as we discussed business matters, I quickly wrote down things he needed me to do. At what I thought was the end of the conversation, I asked, "So, when did you want me to e-mail these numbers to you by?"

"Um . . ." He thought about it. "I need the sales information no later than noon tomorrow, and everything else just send to me as you get it, no rush."

"Okay." I gave my computer mouse a shake to get back to work. "I'll try to get the sales analogy to you before I leave today."

"See, Garcelle?" he chuckled. "That's why they pay you the big bucks."

"They do?" I asked jokingly.

"You do great work, so I know that you're getting paid over there," he said. "When I come to Chicago, you'll have to show me that lavish mansion you live in."

"Ha!" I laughed. "Sure, but give me enough time to have the maids do a thorough cleaning."

"Is four days enough time?" he asked.

"Oh, yeah." I went on painting the bogus picture. "Yes, that will give me enough time to have the silver polished and pool cleaned, too. Even though it's too cold to take a dip, I need to have the leaves removed," I said in my best *Lifestyles of the Rich and Famous* voice.

"Not a problem," he said, and then asked, "So, are you free this Friday night?"

"Yes, as a matter of fact I am." I smiled.

Cortez asked, "How about dinner?"

I continued jokingly, "Sure, have your people call my people, they'll send a car for you."

"Oh, no," he chuckled. "No, I'm being serious now."

"What do you mean?" I dropped the pen.

I held my breath as he answered, "My friend Mark in Chicago is getting married on Saturday, so I'm flying in on Friday morning and leaving on Sunday."

"Oh, so you want to meet the staff while you're here?" I asked.

"The staff?" He clarified, "No, just you. I was hoping to finally meet you in person while I was there." He paused. "If that's okay."

"Um." I was flabbergasted, and took at least five seconds to get it together. "Sure."

"Wait, Garcelle!" He paused. "You don't sound too sure. There's no pressure here. I mean, I don't even know your situation, so if I'm out of line for asking, please let me know."

"No, it's fine." I was tickled hot pink as I continued. "You just caught me off guard, that's all."

"Sorry about that," Cortez said. "Since we talk and e-mail so much, I feel like I know you, so it would be a pleasure to put a face to the name."

I agreed, "Same here."

There was an awkward silence before he said, "I won't be in the office on Thursday, and I don't know if I'll have time to call again before Friday, so may I have another number to reach you when I'm there?"

"Sure."

We exchanged phone numbers, said our good-byes, and as the receiver touched its cradle, I was already on Google, typing *3 days to lose weight*. A million links appeared about a diet called the Three Day Diet. A person should lose ten pounds in three days, but there was no concrete evidence or information on whether it truly worked.

While I was online, I visited the Blare Corporation Web site again. I had stolen a few glances of a picture of Cortez on the company's Web site before, but now I had to do it again. He was the color of a freshly polished oak floor, and was incredibly handsome with a white boy nose and thin, yet suckable, Tyson Beckford lips. He was tall, built, and had titillating light brown eyes that I couldn't even look at on the screen without feeling some kind of way.

"Knock knock." Into my office walked Jason with purple African violets in a Styrofoam cup. "This is for you, pretty lady."

"Thank you." I took the flowers, smiled, and pretended not to know that the city of Chicago had African violets arranged beautifully in large pots at every El train station. "That was thoughtful," I said.

He leaned in my doorway. "How was your weekend?"

"It was okay," I said. "And yours?"

"It was cool. I didn't do much," he said. "I couldn't really get you off my mind, though."

"Really?" I asked, and wondered if the free drinks had anything to do with it.

"Yeah, you're an amazing kisser," he whispered. "I thought about that shit the entire weekend."

I offered him a genuine smile. "Thank you," I said, but found myself wondering what it might be like to kiss Cortez.

"Think there's a chance we can do that again?" he asked. "You know, going out and kicking it, and possibly another kiss?"

"We'll see," I said.

"Wow." Jason took a step back. "You shuttin' me down like that?"

"No, I wasn't saying it like that," I lied. "I just meant we'll have to wait and see what happens the next time, ya know?"

"Yeah." He smiled. "Well, we get paid this Friday, so I should have a li'l something to play with and be able to do it right this time. You free on Friday night?"

"Actually, I just made plans to have dinner with a friend from out of town on Friday." I wasn't lying.

"No problem." He seemed disappointed. "Well, stop by my area before you leave today if you can. Okay?"

"Okay," I said. "Thanks again for the flowers."

"No need to thank me, all thanks to you." He winked. "See ya."

Jason didn't seem like a bad guy, just an average guy with below-average judgment and little drive. Those were all things that could be enhanced if he so chose, so I was willing to be cordial with him until he got himself together. However, on my way to say good-bye to him, I spotted a floral arrangement identical to mine in a much nicer blue Solo cup on Leslie's desk, and decided that Jason wasn't worth any more than the pot he didn't have to piss in. I turned toward the exit, and heard the frosty wind howl as I approached the door. I bundled up in my coat, and pulled my hat on tight, because it would be a shame for this human-hair-lace-front wig to be found on the Dan Ryan in the accident lane clinging to life.

"What's up, chica?" Stacy's voice resonated in my Bluetooth earpiece.

"Nothing much. What's going on with you?" I said as I turned onto the highway. "Anything crazy happen today?"

"Something crazy always happens at Rush." I loved hearing all of her emergency room nurse tales. "A man came in this morning with a TV remote control in his rectum."

I thought about it, then gasped. "What the . . ." I exploded into laughter. "Ew." I nearly choked.

"You see everything in the ER." Stacy giggled. "You name it and I've seen it."

I had to know. "Was he masturbating?" I asked.

"No, Garcelle, he stumbled and fell on it." She laughed. "Of course he was masturbating."

"Shut up!" I smiled.

"He was trying to TiVo himself," she joked. "So, how is a day in the life of the senior reports director at Blare?"

"Ha-ha, don't let the e-mail signature fool you, darling. I'm only senior because I'm the only damn one." I clarified, "The only one doing the work of three."

"Aw, poor baby," Trace teased. "Why don't you get them to hire someone else?"

"Because then I won't have a job. They'll find out that it takes me almost no time to do what I do." I giggled. "I get my work done mostly before lunch every day, and then I shop online and play *Second Life* the rest of the time."

"That's just trifling," Stacy said. "I bet your boss—"

"Oh," I interrupted her. "Speaking of bosses, remember that guy Cortez I was telling you about who works at our home office?"

"Yeah, in Jacksonville, right?" she asked.

"Yeah, yeah." My voice went up an octave in excitement. "Well, he called me today to go over some changes, and, at the end of the conversation, he told me that he was coming here this weekend and wants to take me out to dinner."

"Whoa!" she exclaimed. "I assume you said yes?"

"I did," I said uncertainly, "but, honestly, I don't know what I'm going to do."

"What?" She tried to figure out what the problem was. "What, you don't know what to wear?"

"No," I whined. "I wish it were that simple." I laid out my dilemma. "As far as I know, Cortez has never seen me; he's just inviting me out based on our conversations. What if I'm physically not his type?"

Stacy chuckled. "So, you wanna burn a man at the stake because he's willing to get to know you based on your personality rather than your looks?"

"No." I fought to explain. "What I mean is what if he has high physical expectations, or is looking for something different?"

"Looking for something like what?" Stacy asked.

"Something like, like . . ." I thought. "Like you, a damn size six and not me, an eighteen, a sixteen in the summer months," I said.

"Oh, Garcelle, stop it," she scolded me. "You act like you're the biggest woman in Chicago." She went on. "You don't even look like an eighteen, and if you don't like it, then you know what to do to change it."

"Well, I'm gonna try this three-day diet thing I read about online," I said. "I'm starting tomorrow, and, hopefully, by Friday I will have lost a little something."

Stacy probably didn't know much about my smoke-and-mirrors technique. It is said that magicians often use smoke and mirrors during their acts to conceal things that would give a trick away. Well, I did the same thing with Spanx, duct tape, Body Magic, two bras at once, etc. You name it and I've probably tried it. Nearly took my nipple off with duct tape, but it did do the trick. I just didn't know how to get it off without my skin following.

"A three-day diet, Garcelle?" I could tell she was rolling her eyes. "I've invited you to my gym countless times."

"Stacy, your gym is like a club. Men are posted up on the walls watching women with hardly anything on, there are down-low brothers stalking the bathroom stalls, fights in the parking lot, and drag queens on the treadmills." I laughed. "What the hell? That's just too much drama for me. I want a simple gym, preferably one without a DJ booth." I laughed.

"You are too silly." Stacy cracked up. "Enough about that, what are you gonna do about Friday?"

"Well," I sighed, "I plan to go, but if I don't hear from him before noon or so on Friday, I'm probably going to do something else."

"Something else like what?" Stacy called me out. "You don't have anything else to do on Friday night but call and bother me when I'm trying to conceive!" she reminded me. "I should be ovulating on Friday, so please don't think you're coming over."

"You are such a skank," I said.

"Whatever," she replied. "At least give him until about five to call if he's traveling on Friday; he might have stuff to do. Damn, have a heart."

"I guess," I stubbornly agreed. "I'll give him until five, and then I'm crashing the ovulation party," I joked. "Nah, I hope this is it this time."

"Me too," she said. "Keep your fingers crossed, again."

While she discussed her adventures of trying to conceive, my mind drifted off to the last time I had had sex. It had been months and months by choice, not by accident. After Mitch left my place that hot August night, I made a vow to put my pussy on ice for a year. However, I think I was ready to release it on six months' time served.

Mitch was a guy I had met at the supermarket. We passed each other in several aisles. He saw the puzzled look on my face as I searched for a can of San Marzano crushed tomatoes, an ingredient to make Paula Deen's eggplant parmesan. "May I help you find something?" he asked.

"Huh?" I looked him up and down. He wasn't wearing the store uniform. "Do you work here?"

"No, but it looks like you need help finding something," he said. "Two heads are better than one."

"Well, I'm looking for a can of San Marzano crushed tomatoes," I said.

He scanned the cans, then stopped. "I don't know if they carry San Marzano, but what about Heinz?"

"I guess that will have to do," I said, as he reached down for the can. "Thank you."

He introduced himself as Mitchell Williams, and asked me to call him Mitch. We exchanged numbers, talked that night, and texted a lot over the next week or so. The night I had planned to make my eggplant parmesan, I invited him over. He showed up on time and ready to eat . . . me. Our text messages had become increasingly sexual, but I didn't expect Mitch to literally, as his messages said, pick me up and put me on my dining room table to devour my tasty treat moments after walking through the door.

"Wait a minute," I said, trying to get off the table.

"I told you that I was eating this pussy straight out the gate, didn't I?" he asked.

"Yeah, but I thought you were kidding," I said, as he reached between my dangling legs, pushed past my thick thighs, and landed on my panties. "Are you serious?"

"Yes." He pressed my shoulders down until my back was against the table. He rubbed my clit through my underwear and groaned. "I've been thinking about this since that day in the store."

He pulled my panties down and spread open my legs, getting a good look at my chocolate-covered peach as he rubbed himself through his jeans. "Damn, that looks good." He pulled my ass to the edge of the table and fell to his knees.

"Wait." I tried to sit up, but his strong hand pushed down on my chest.

"Let me take care of this for you," he said. "I will only go as far as you want." He let up on my chest. "Relax."

Of course, I could've stopped him, but a part of me felt guilty for encouraging him via text message the way I did. He started lapping my juicy puckering lips like a thirsty dog. I ground my honey pit into his tongue and then he started to drill me slowly with it. I worked his tongue like a stripper on a pole, but he moved with me and grooved me into ecstasy. He stood up with a condom over his dick and slid into me, or, at least, I thought he had. He was making all the motions and shaking the table, but I couldn't feel a thing.

As he moaned and groaned, I thought of the chocolate raspberry cheesecake recipe I saw in Paula's cookbook, then I thought I heard the table crack. "Stop." I squeezed him around the waist with my knees. "Let's get on the floor."

Mitch lay on the floor and I straddled him. His dick "on hard" looked smaller than the average man's did without an erection. I rolled my eyes and just bounced on it. "Oh, yeah, baby," he called out, and grabbed my hands. "Fuck that big dick." I wanted to laugh, and I probably could've, because his eyes were shut real tight. "Choke me." He put my hands on his neck.

I was caught off guard. "What?"

"Just squeeze me real tight."

"No," I said. "I'm not into that."

"I am." He pushed up fast and hard as if he actually thought his dick was making it close to anything in me that mattered. "If you do it, it'll make me cum real fast."

Okay, choking it is! I squeezed my hands around his neck, and he opened his eyes. I was trying not to apply too much pressure, but his rocking under me made my hands jerk back and forth on his throat. When his eyes rolled back and he stopped moving, I stopped. "Mitch?" He didn't respond. "Mitch?" I called a second time, and, as soon as I started to panic, he turned his head to the side and vomited on my carpet.

"What the fuck?" I screamed, and jumped up.

"Damn, that was good," he said, stretching as if he had woken from a dream. He looked over at the yellowish goo on my rug. "Shit, I should've told you about that," he said nonchalantly. "Get me a towel."

"No, get the hell out." I was sick of being nice. I let him fuck me because I didn't know how to say no. "Please leave." No more Miss Niceness.

"I can clean it up," he offered again.

"No, thanks." I pulled my dress down. "Just go." Within a minute, I was closing the door behind Mr. Choke Me 'Til I Puke. Since that day, I had decided to use better judgment when it came to sex and not just give in because there was a dick in the room. I knew nothing about Mitch, other than what he said his last name was, his cell number, and that he liked to text freakiness. After he left, I realized how dangerous the situation have been and put myself on a year-long sex fast. But after six months, I was convinced that I had learned my lesson.

On Friday, in typical "overdoing it" style, I called out from work, and was in my beautician's chair at 8:00 A.M. and out at 12:30 P.M. To follow up, I stopped by my usual salon off Ninety-fifth and Western and got a fresh mani/pedi. And last, but not least, I found a plum, colored deep V-neck wrap dress with accessories to wear. I was on my way home when my phone rang. My heart practically jumped out and hit the brake pedal when I saw Cortez's name.

"Hello!" I tried to sound unfazed.

"Hey, this is Cortez," he replied. "How are you?"

"Oh, hi. I'm fine." I faked it. "How was your flight?"

"It was okay until my bag went missing," he said.

"Oh, no," I gasped.

"Well, the airline says it's delayed, but it still hasn't made it to my hotel, so to me, it's lost." He chuckled.

"I'm so sorry." I felt bad for him. "Well, we don't have to meet up, since you have that going on."

"Are you kidding? I already bought something to put on tonight just in case they don't get here before you do." He then checked. "That is, of course, if you're still interested in joining me for dinner."

"I am." I paused. "But I've lost bags during traveling before and it's a pain, and I know that you probably want to stick around the hotel to be there when they get there and make sure that all of your items are accounted for."

"You're right about that," he said. "So, I was going to ask you if you would mind if we just stayed around the hotel. Heard the food in the restaurant is excellent."

"Which hotel are you at?" I had to know because I had had a few bad experiences.

"The W on Lakeshore Drive," he replied. "I checked in about an hour ago and have a view of the lake. Even though it's frozen, it's real nice to look at."

"So, Mr. Sunshine, how are you dealing with this weather? Tell me your coat wasn't in your checked bag."

"No, I brought it on with me because I know that that Chicago hawk is no joke, that wind is serious," he said. "Oh, and by the way, I haven't always been a Floridian. I was born and raised in Cleveland. I moved to Miami ten years ago and moved north to Jacksonville four years ago, so I know about shoveling snow and all that. I'm just glad I don't have to do it anymore."

"How lucky you are," I said.

"So . . ." He cleared his throat. "I don't want to ask this, but then again, I've put off asking you this for so long already." Cortez paused. "Who shovels your snow?"

I assumed this was his way of asking if I had a man. "Well, I live in a condo on the ninth floor, so the only snow I have to worry about is on my car." I laughed. "I can handle that."

"Garcelle, you're making this hard," he said. "Do you have a boyfriend, husband, a man, or anything like that?" he boldly asked.

"No, I'm single," I said with a smile.

"Okay, because the crime rate in Chicago is bananas and I don't want to become a statistic taking you out."

I was all blushed out. "So, what time should I be there?" I asked.

"What time is good for you?" He put the ball back in my court.

I looked at the clock. "Eight would work for me."

"Then eight it is," he said. "I'll be at the bar."

"Sounds good." I smiled and checked my rearview mirror to get over to the right.

"I'll see you then," he said.

"See ya." I released the call and my palms were moist. I couldn't believe that I was doing this.

I got home, jumped into the shower, and hoped that my nervousness would wash away with the soap, but it didn't. My nerves actually helped me put on my dress, makeup, and shoes. As a matter of fact, it drove with me all the way down to 644 North Lake Shore Drive. When I pulled up to the valet, it really woke up. "Good evening, ma'am." The driver politely reached in to help me out.

I stepped out into the night, which was accompanied by the frozen lakefront air, and my exposed legs that became thick chocolate popsicles because my coat was mid-length. I raced out of the weather and into the lobby only to find myself wanting to run back out of the door. To say I was apprehensive would be an understatement; I was petrified. I hoped to God that he didn't have anything against a bigger woman.

"Hi, can you please point me to the bar?" I grinned and asked one of the ladies at the front desk.

"Sure." The tall pale woman pointed. "Right around that corner."

"Thank you," I said, and forced my feet from going in the opposite direction. As I turned the corner, I saw several men sitting at the bar, but only two were black and only one made my entire body water. He was wearing black slacks and a beige sweater, and had short wavy hair and a silky goatee. He was turned sideways, looking up at the forty-two-inch plasma television airing a basketball game on *ESPN*. I was about ten feet away when he must have felt me staring and did a double take in my direction. And even with my two-sizes-too-big felt coat on, he didn't look disgusted or let down. His face actually lit up, or was it the way the bar's light cast on him as he stood? Either way, he looked more handsome than he did just two seconds before.

"Garcelle?" he asked softly.

"Yes." I smiled. "Hello, Cortez!"

"Well, hello, you." He took me by the hand and pulled me into a quick, innocent embrace. "How are you?"

"I'm great," I lied. "How are you?" I asked as we let go of each other. "Has your bag come yet?"

"No." He laughed. "It's not looking good, so I probably won't wear my brand new suit tomorrow at the wedding."

"Oh, no!" I frowned. "Are you in the wedding?" I started unbuttoning my coat.

"No, but I wish I were, then I would have been renting a tux here instead of bringing one. Now, I may have to buy yet another suit."

I threw in my logic. "Well, if the other one is new and you have your receipt, maybe you can take that one back."

"I already had it altered by a tailor outside of the company." Cortez moved behind me to help me out of my coat. "Let me help you with that," he said, as I shivered.

"Thank you," I whispered. Our eyes caught each other when I glanced shyly over my shoulder.

"Mm." His soft baritone made my eardrum tremble. He leaned in closer to me. "You smell amazing," he said, and pulled the coat away from my body.

"Thank you, it's Vera Wang," I said.

"Very nice." He nodded his approval, then gestured at the barstool. "Care to have a drink, or would you like to get started on dinner?"

How absolutely big and fat would I sound if I said we should start on dinner? I smiled. "I would love a cocktail." I sat on the heavy leather chair as he adorned its back with my black felt coat. "What are you having?"

"Whiskey sour," Cortez replied as he waved the bartender over. "What do you feel like?"

"I'll have a Bellini." I smiled.

"A Bellini for the lady," Cortez said to the man, as he sat next to me and turned in my direction, resting his elbow on the bar. "You have such an incredible voice."

"Really?" I blushed. "Thank you!"

"You should do voice-overs," he advised.

He caught me off guard. "Voice-overs?" Oh, he meant incredible voice in *that* way. I thought he meant incredibly sexy, but he meant incredibly marketable. "Thank you."

Over two drinks, our conversation stayed pretty safe. We discussed the weather, things to do in the area, and things related to the business. Even after we strolled over to Wave, the hotel's restaurant, our chat was still very formal, only added to the pot were politics and boxing, which we both were fans of. My grilled free-range chicken with caramelized onions and roasted garlic, and side of macaroni and cheese gratin, had come and were almost gone when he suddenly said, "I didn't expect you to be so . . ." He paused. "There's only one way to put it, so attractive."

My eyes widened to the size of saucers, and I forgot to breathe. "Thank you," I said on my next breath, as my inner self ran around the table screaming cheers of joy.

He drank the last of his four whiskey sours. "I've been fighting the urge to say that since you walked in." He smiled. "I hope that I'm not out of line or unprofessional for saying that."

"Well, we have been talking about work an awful lot," I teased with a smile, "but we aren't at work." I eased his mind.

"Great!" He relaxed. "As I said earlier, your voice is incredible, and your personality over the phone is amazing, but your smile, your skin . . . your beauty is astonishing, and you're single," he said. "It's rare to find all of that in one woman without her being a nutcase," he joked. "So, what's wrong with you?"

"I'm wanted in several states," I teased.

"True," he flirted. "One being Florida."

"Maybe," I said.

"No, certainly," Cortez assured me. "You would be a welcomed attraction in Jacksonville."

"Thank you." My whole body blushed as his commanding brown eyes proved too powerful for me to stare into. "You're a very good-looking guy yourself."

He laughed. "Well, thank you."

"But I had already seen a picture of you on the Blare Web site," I confessed.

"Snoop." He made fun of me.

"So, now, what if I showed up and you didn't find me attractive at all?" I asked.

"There would be no difference in my conversation, generosity, or friendship," he said. "I obviously didn't invite you out based on what you look like. It was because of the great job you do and your personality." He sipped his drink. "The fact that you're a sight for sore eyes is just a bonus."

Though he paid me compliment after compliment, I couldn't help but wonder if he was picturing me fifty pounds lighter and thinking, *Damn, she would be so much finer if she lost some weight.*

"Well, thank you," I said, and then things got quiet.

"Oh, don't get shy on me now," he said. "So, what if you didn't find me to be, as you say, a good-looking guy? Would you have agreed to dinner?"

"Heck no," I joked. "Nah, seriously. I would've still agreed to dinner. After all, you are an executive in the home office who I can bounce ideas off of, get a better understanding of things from, and find out more about the company from. I would consider it a learning experience." It was what I called a beauty pageant answer. It sounded good and would impress the world, but there was no truth to it at all.

Cortez laughed. "A learning experience, huh?"

"Yes," I said. "You can never have too many of those."

"Ugly dates?" He played on my words.

"No." I laughed heavily. "Learning experiences!"

"So," he continued, "why would you say that you're single?"

I was unsure of what to say. "Well, I guess I could be dating if I wanted, but it seems I just keep meeting the same man with a difference face and name." I shook my head. "So I'm on a little sabbatical to see if it's something I'm doing to keep attracting the wrong men."

He laughed. "I don't think you're doing anything wrong." He gave me a hungry once-over. "I mean, look at you. Any man would be honored to have you on his arm."

I didn't want to say anything to seem unsure of myself, but out it came anyway. "Well, you know that most men like women who are more on the, how can I say?" I thought carefully because I didn't want to sound like a hater. "Women on the size-two side."

"Size two?" He grinned. "Nah, the only thing a size two can do for me is hang around in case I lose my key. She can slip through the keyhole and open the door." He laughed. "I like a woman who looks and feels like a woman. I need curves and shape."

If I were pale, I would've gone red in the face. "Well, it's certainly good to know that you know how to appreciate a real woman."

He gawked at me across the table from the waist up and then down again. "You are definitely real, a real beauty."

"Thank you," I said. The flattery was great, but I didn't want him to get too cheesy. I changed the subject. "So, what's wrong with *you*?" I questioned. "Why are you single?"

"Well." He cleared his throat. "I'm actually newly divorced."

Oh, God! This piece of information I didn't know. Was he one of those divorced men who was free and looking to fuck any and everything in a skirt? Or was he the kind who was now bitter toward women because one had basically made him feel like a failure? Did he have kids? How long had he been married? Oh, God . . . I could smell the drama coming. "How long were you married?"

"Four years," he answered. "I know what your next question is. I have no children."

"Okay!" I breathed a nonchalant sigh of relief. "How long have you been divorced?"

"Well, we were separated for a year and a half, but the divorce has been final now for about five months."

"Sorry that things didn't work out." I was at a loss for words.

"It's cool," he said. "You live and learn."

"So, what did you learn?" I asked.

"Ha!" He sat back in his chair. "I learned that getting married because you're sick of arguing about not being married is not the right route."

Over another round of drinks at the dinner table, he told me the story of his failed marriage, unsuccessful business they started, and two miscarriages. He didn't seem hurt, bitter, or nostalgic about his wife; he truly seemed as though he was over it and ready to move on.

"Can you see yourself getting married again?" I asked.

"Mm. Good question," he said, and sipped his drink again. "I can see it, but it won't be anytime soon. She would have to have something to bring to the table, and not just show up expecting to have everything supplied for her." He thought for a moment and continued. "The chemistry can't be questionable; we have to be best friends."

"Sounds good." I didn't know how to answer without sounding like I wanted to audition for the part of wife number two. "Good luck."

"No, no, no luck." Cortez chuckled. "I don't want another woman who is lucky to have me. I want to be considered a blessing to someone."

"I hear that," I said.

He looked at his watch as if he had something else to do and was about to call it a night, but surprisingly, he said, "So, the night is still young. Would you like to do something else?"

"Something else?" I repeated the question. "Something like what?"

He shrugged his shoulders. "This is your town; you were supposed to come with an itinerary." He laughed, and then recalled, "What was the tall building you were telling me about before?"

"The Hancock Building?" I asked.

"Yes," he said. "As many times as I have visited here, I have never been there."

"Well, we can go there if you want. On the ninety-sixth floor is a lounge with an unbelievable view."

"I bet," he said. "Maybe we can do that tomorrow night?"

"Tomorrow night?" I asked in shock.

"Yeah." He signed his receipt, and then apologized. "I'm sorry, you probably have plans."

"I'm free tomorrow night." I blushed. "I'm sure you'll enjoy the view."

"I'm already enjoying it," he said. He stood and stared down at me. "And it's breathtaking." He reached down for my hand.

"Thank you." I smiled. "So, where are we about to go?"

"I was going to suggest a walk, but it's negative two hundred degrees outside." He laughed. "So, I can speak with the concierge and see what's happening in the area tonight, and we can take a cab. Is that okay?"

"Sure." It had been a long time since I had been out and truly enjoyed myself with a guy. He was nothing like the last few trifling men I had gone out with. Like Jason, for example. What kind of foolishness was that? Some men felt that because a woman had a few extra pounds to carry, they wouldn't mind carrying their sorry grown asses around, too, but I didn't have the strength or tolerance for all of that dead weight.

After a few minutes of speaking to the concierge, he turned to me and said, "I know it's cold outside, but how about a horse and carriage ride to Hole in the Wall?" he reluctantly asked.

"Are you sure you won't be cold?"

"I should be okay as long as you sit close enough." He ushered me into a hug.

"I'll see what I can do." I grinned.

Fifteen minutes later, a breathtakingly sturdy black satin stallion pulling an eggshell-colored carriage galloped up to the street in front of the hotel. Cortez stood. "Ready?"

"Let's go." I smiled. I had never taken advantage of seeing the city by horse and carriage. It was already looking even better.

Cortez helped me into the carriage as the driver looked at

us and asked if we were celebrating anything special. I shook my head when I heard Cortez say, "It's our first date."

"Lovely!" the man replied. "So, will there be a second one?"

"I think so," he answered, and looked over at me. "Will there be a third?" he asked, putting me on the spot.

"I don't see why not." My cheeks were flushed. "But the night is still young," I joked.

Cortez paid the driver and adjusted his scarf before sitting down. "This is nice." He looked around the plush coach.

I was awestruck! "Wow," I said, as I looked up and around downtown Chicago. We slowly trotted down Ontario Street. "This is amazing," I said. "I mean, I've been down this street a million times, but it's so different this way."

He interrupted, "It's the night air, the smell, the sounds of the city; it makes a big difference."

"Yes, it does." I sat up in my seat a bit, and fell silent for a few minutes as I took in my Windy City.

"Are you cold?" Cortez asked, breaking the silence.

I was hardly paying attention. "Huh?"

"Cold?" he asked, staring down at my exposed legs.

"A little, but I'm from here," I said. "The question is are *you* cold?"

"I'm glad you asked," he answered with a mischievous grin. "I'm freezing, but I think if you sat just a little closer, it would help my situation."

"You think so?" I nestled closer to him. "How's that?"

"I still feel a chill." He pretended to tremble. "Come closer."

I put my hand on his kneecap and pulled myself even nearer to him. "How's this?"

"Great, thank you!" His strong hand caressed my arm through my jacket. My heartbeat mirrored the click-clacking of the horse's hooves. A thick quiet fell between us. Not the type where no one has anything to say, but the kind where there is so much to say that no one wants to say it first. What did I want to say? In a million ways, I wanted to tell him just how much I was enjoying his company. I cuddled up to him again; his chest was firm and his fragrance delicious. "I cannot believe that we're doing this." He pointed at himself and then me.

"I know." I held his arm.

He said, "After all this time on the phone, e-mailing you, and being curious about you."

"What were you curious about?" I turned into an investigative reporter.

"I wondered if you were single, married, or had kids," he said. "I wondered what you looked like, smelled like, felt like." We both fell silent and rode the rest of the ride that way.

We were seated at a tiny table in a dimly lit, smoke-filled Hole in the Wall, listening to a jazz band get down. I pinched myself to see if any of this was real, and, just then, he reached across the table and stroked my hand. Minutes later, he pulled me to the dance floor and we danced like we owned the joint. Afterward, we drank coffee and shared a slice of chocolate-and-raspberry cheesecake, my favorite.

It was after midnight when we stood in the lobby pretending that we could just say good-bye and pick up where we left off another time. On the third hug, Cortez asked, "Why don't you just come up?"

"Well," I said, smiling, "because you haven't asked."

"Oh." He raised his eyebrows. "Is that all I need to do?"

"Maybe," I teased.

"Well, Miss Monroe." He pulled me into him. "Will you join me in my room upstairs?"

"Sure." I winked at him. "I would have ten minutes ago."

We decided to have one more round of drinks before going up. His phone chimed while we were at the bar. He said it was Bill from my office, so he walked to the restroom, on the phone, and I used the time to freshen my makeup. My last drink was a Long Island Iced Tea. What a mistake. It pushed me over the line of buzz to drunk, and it was a full moon, so I was horny! I wasn't cum-in-my-face-'cause-I'm-a-dirty-whore horny, I was I-really-want-him-to-at-least-rub-me-through-my-panties horny, but times three. I had no business being in close proximity to a man so sexually appealing under these circumstances.

When we got to the room, he asked, "Would you like to watch something or listen to some music? What would you like to do?"

"What would I like to do?" I repeated tauntingly, as I stumbled to the bed. "I could think of a million things I could do in this room." At this very moment, Jamie Foxx's "Blame It" would start playing on the soundtrack of my life. "Mm, so much to do, starting with you."

His eyes jumped open. "Me?"

"Yes, you." I kicked off my shoes. "Come here." I beckoned him to the bed. "Let's see what you're working with." Yes, I actually said that. It was a line straight out of the Ghetto Trick Hall of Fame. What was I doing? I had never even thought of saying that to a man. Insert chorus to Jamie's song here.

"What?" He laughed it off.

Instead of leaving well enough alone, I continued. "Please don't tell me that you like men."

"Men?" His smile was gone when he turned to look at me. "I think that over the course of this evening, I've shown you several times what I like."

"Why are you all the way over there then?" I mumbled as I made the short trek over to where he was standing. I held on to him to keep standing. "And why are you wearing all these clothes?" the Long Island Iced Tea in me asked. "Let's get you comfy." I removed his coat and dress shirt. He was wearing a T-shirt that exposed the definition in his arms, and that excited me. "Oh, I would love to see your chest."

Cortez obliged, unveiling his solid chest and abs. I raked my fingers across his abs and loved it. I would be in a coffin for a year before my stomach was that flat. "Very nice," I said as my hands traveled up to his chest, where I circled his nipple and moved in for a kiss. Our lips touched and had a heated conversation of their own. His lips were soft and sweet. After several long pecks, there was no pulling us apart. He passionately guided my tongue into his mouth, as a snake charmer would a snake, and drew it gently into his warmth, but I wanted more and fast. I abandoned his lips and left a sensual trail of kisses on his cheek. I traveled down his neck, onto his chest, stopped at his nipple, and encircled it with my tongue.

"Whoa, whoa!" He backed away. "Wait. What are you doing?"

"Come back and let me show you," I teased. "Come here."

"I better not." He shook his head. "I think I gave you the wrong impression. I'm not interested in having sex with you."

"Oh." The sober parts within me were embarrassed. "I just thought—"

"Excuse me. I need to use the restroom," he cut me off, and walked away.

I felt like a complete idiot. I had sucked on the nipple of the man who was my boss' boss, and he flat out shut me down. He had done nothing wrong. In fact, he was probably trying to save us from a professional headache, but I didn't see it like that. My mind plagued me with thoughts that he didn't find me attractive or wasn't interested in me sexually. There was no way I was staying around for more. I grabbed my coat and brown Coach purse, and was on the elevator before he came out.

As I headed south on Lake Shore Drive, my phone began

to sing; it was Cortez. I reached for it, but there was no way I was going to explain to him the things going on in my mind. He would think I was crazy, extremely insecure, slutty or all three. Sure, I had some things I was insecure about; we all have things about ourselves we would love to change. I shielded my body as if it were a government secret. However, when it all boiled down to it, when the time was right with a man, I couldn't hide anything, naked was naked, but I knew how to use smoke and mirrors in a candlelit room.

Cortez called four times over and over, but I never answered. Instead, I called Stacy. Bobby picked up, sounding half-asleep. "Hello?"

"Oh, shit," I said under my breath when I realized the time. "I'm so sorry to call so late, Bobby. I guess she's asleep, huh?"

"Yeah," he grumbled. "You want me to get her up?"

"Nah," I said. "It can wait."

"You sure?" He was concerned. "Are you okay? You need something?"

"Yeah, I'm fine," I said. "I just didn't know what time it was. It's nothing serious. I'll call back tomorrow."

"All right!" He yawned. "Be safe."

"Thanks." I hung up.

For a split second, I missed Noriah, our other friend. We fell out a year ago when she accused me of wanting to sleep with her husband. It all started when I became a member on this swinger's site for black people. I didn't know what I was looking for or expecting. I got the idea because Michael Baisden always talked about it on his radio show. I just wanted to talk to people in the lifestyle and learn how this type of relationship worked. It only took two days for my inbox to be full after I added a picture of my boobs.

A guy who called himself Stamina4dayz wrote me and I wrote back. He sent me pictures of him below the waist and I was very pleased. We corresponded on Yahoo! Messenger for days.

He said he was single and looking for a single female swing partner to have full swaps with other couples. I told him that I was new to the lifestyle and was just looking to slowly be introduced, or maybe just watch. We never exchanged numbers, just IMed every so often. After about a month, he wanted to meet me, so I suggested drinks at Bar Louise in Hyde Park.

I was at the bar at nine on a Saturday night. He knew I would be wearing a red sweater, and he told me to be on the lookout for a six-foot, seven-inch, 250-pound dude in a Chicago White Sox fleece pullover. On the first sip of my second glass of Riesling, I saw Eric walk through the door in Sox gear, but didn't make the connection; after all, we lived in Chicago. I hid my face with a menu because I didn't want Eric coming over to say hi and never leaving when my company showed up. I then received a Yahoo message alert on my phone. "I'm here!"

"Me, too!" I wrote back.

He then asked, "Where are you?"

"At the bar, red sweater, below the margarita sign." I sent my message.

Less than ten seconds later, there was a touch on my back, and I turned around to Eric's hand. He looked like he wanted to faint. "Garcelle?"

"Eric?" I said in shock. "You're Stamina?"

"Damn." He hung his head. "Damn."

I thought of how Noriah was always bragging about her perfect relationship. "Wow!" I said, looking away from him.

He was right behind me and in my ear. "Let's pretend this never happened, please," he begged.

I turned to look at him, and heard, "So, this is what the fuck y'all been doing?" Noriah yelled from behind him. "You're cheating on me with this fat bitch?" She slapped him several times in the face. "This is what you on, Eric? This is what the fuck you on, you punk bitch?" She tried to punch at me, but Eric pushed her back. She fell onto some man, spilling his drink, which fueled another commotion, and we were all put out; security escorted me to my car. Noriah had apparently seen our chats on Eric's phone while he was sleeping earlier, and followed him out of the house to see who he was meeting and cheating with.

During my short ride, I tried calling Noriah, but she didn't pick up. However, before I even got home, I received a text that went out to everyone in her contacts: Garcelle Monroe is a nasty, sneaky, dick-hungry whore who is out to fuck any man her fat ass can get. Reading that was like injecting poison into me, it was killing me. I was so hurt that I didn't give a damn about explaining things to her anymore. A few days later, Stacy spoke to her on my behalf. She told Stacy that she felt we had both been jealous of her relationship, and she wanted nothing else to do with either of us.

So, our three was now only two. When I couldn't talk to Stacy, I talked to no one. Now, rushing home from the hotel, I wished I had someone to cry to. Instead, I got home, crawled under the sheets, and recapped my evening with Cortez. It seemed like things had been going well. He expressed interest in me outside of the professional realm. He said I was beautiful, and loved my personality, so when he invited me back to his room, naturally, I assumed it was an open invitation to feast on his twenty-four-hour buffet. Then, like a badly made movie, my chest-licking scene played in my mind, and I cringed in disgust.

Cortez wasn't just some guy I met at a bar, and I couldn't ignore him forever. Though I might never see him again, I would probably hear from him on Monday morning, and although it would be about work, it would be awkward. I was hoping that the weekend would take my cares away before Monday.

***

On Saturday, my *Second Life* sorority, Alpha Phi Kappa, was set to cross a new pledge line, so when I logged into my account at 9:00 A.M., I stayed on my laptop until well after midnight. *Second Life* is a 3-D virtual world online where you can do anything, and when I say anything, I mean anything. You build your character or avatar to look like whatever or whomever you like, and once you learn your way around and meet the right people, *Second Life* could be extremely fun and addictive. It's a place to do things you can't or won't do in real life. I had always wanted to be in a sorority, and there I had the opportunity. It felt so good to do the things we do that I regretted not pledging in college. Though it was all virtual, my twenty-seven sisters and I shared a true sisterhood. And though our Greek letters, AΦK, and chapter information couldn't be found on any college campus, we took our vows very seriously.

My sorors and I have step shows, and wear and represent our colors: chocolate, purple, and pink. We raise money for real life charities, have virtual garage sales, recruit new members, and throw the bomb parties. My entire Saturday was spent in the house because I was pledge master in AΦK, and had to help my sisters finish building the ceremonial platform, attend the crossing ceremony, and, immediately after, entertain a crowd at the crossing ball, all in *Second Life*. You'd have to see it to believe. Stunna76, one of our associated frat brothers, was my date for the event. He went all out picking me up in a limo, giving me a dozen roses, and a pair of the newest Stiletto Moody shoes (which cost $7,500 in virtual cash and amounts to about twenty-five dollars in real money). Not bad at all; twenty-five was even a good pair of shoes at Payless.

At times, I felt like my virtual life was more exciting than my real life. In *Second Life*, I owned land, a seven-bedroom mansion with perfect landscaping, countless cars and motorcycles, and furniture I couldn't even get on layaway in real life. My avatar was honey brown, six feet tall, 170 pounds soaking wet, had wavy black hair to her butt, ten perfect full faces of makeup to snap on, and shoes galore, with a wardrobe I'd have to beg, borrow, steal, and kill to have in real life. I have been pregnant twice in my virtual world. My "daughter" no longer plays the game, and my "son," in his real life, is going for his master's and only logs on once a month due to being busy with school. They both played teenagers in the game and lived in my house. So, now, I had an empty nest and was single and ready to mingle. I was dating, but just like anywhere, you had your weirdoes, users, and losers, but in *Second Life*, if things didn't go right, I would simply fake a system failure and fix it so that he wouldn't see me logged in again for a while. I loved *Second Life*; it allowed me to have a life when I wanted to escape my real life. Not many people knew about this virtual wonderland, and I liked it that way.

On Sunday, I spent some time at my parents' house. My mom baked macaroni, and, as I did as a kid, I had my plate and fork ready and my hand on the oven door five minutes before the buzzer went off.

"I'm joining Weight Watchers," Mom said.

"For what?" I asked her. "Momma, you don't need to lose any more weight, you look fine."

"I told her that," Daddy said, as he looked at her rear while she fixed his plate. "I like it just like that."

"Daddy!" I yelled to get his attention. "All that was so unnecessary and nasty."

"Leonard, what did you do?" Mom giggled as she asked.

My face was balled up. "He was looking at your butt when he said that." I rolled my eyes at him.

"Well, if he didn't like it, then you wouldn't be here, baby."

"Oh my God. Gimmie the foil, Barry," I said to my brother. "I'm taking my food to go. I can't be around this." I laughed.

We all gathered around the table, prayed, and ate. We had a great time laughing, reminiscing, and even shedding a few tears together. Before leaving for the evening, I told Mom that I might possibly join her on Weight Watchers if the diet I had planned to start the next day didn't work.

Monday came, and all the hustle and bustle of the first day of Blare's new Race to Results Fitness Contest took Cortez completely off my mind. The three-month challenge happened twice a year in the office, and it appeared to be serious business. So much so that when you went to be weighed in, you had to wear the assigned "Race to Results" company T-shirt. All this was since last year when Sarah McCall allegedly had eight bottles of water taped around her waist and lost twenty pounds the first week. I never joined one before. I always laughed about how fanatic everyone got, but, this time, I planned to be a part of the madness. In my tacky, too-tight tee, I ventured to the company's gym to weigh in with Lena, the personal trainer hired to take our measurements, give us tips, and weigh us weekly. Lena and her zero percent body fat couldn't be perkier, more perfect, and any more on my last nerves. One look at Lena's legs in her spandex sickened me. I was hatin' big time, but I couldn't fault her for taking care of her body; I had the same opportunities.

She weighed me, and the scale was merciful; it said 219.5, which was a half pound less than I thought I was. I told Lena about my plan to stay away from meat, fish, bread, and other starches starting the following week for about two weeks. She said that I didn't have to do anything that drastic, but I told her that I wanted to. Lena told me to check with my doctor, and advised me of other good sources of protein since I wouldn't be eating meat. She and I got to talking, and it turned out she wasn't an evil skinny bitch after all. I left the room feeling encouraged and not scorned, taught and not scolded. Halfway back to my office, I realized that the information she had written down was left in the room. When I returned, Sandra, talking on her cell phone, was waiting outside of Lena's door. Sandra was about five foot six and 140 pounds with her kids on her back, so I assumed she was only in the challenge for the weekly gift bags.

I stood a few feet away from her, and wasn't trying to eavesdrop, but she was the only thing to hear in the area. "I'm certainly glad that you didn't miss your flight to Jacksonville." Sandra smiled into the phone. "Just remember what Mark said during the garter toss." She cracked up laughing, as I found myself suddenly trying to crack a case. *Did she just say something about a flight to Jacksonville and refer to a groom as Mark?* "Oh," she went on, "consider yourself lucky. When they lost my brother's luggage, he didn't get it for two weeks."

I found it hard to contain myself. The coincidences were astounding. She had to be talking to . . . "Cortez, I'll call you this evening." She paused to giggle. "I promise it'll be the first thing I do when I walk through the door." Sandra smiled. "TTYL." *Who says that? Isn't that ridiculous shit restricted to text messages and IM?* "See ya, Cort."

I was stunned, embarrassed, and hurt! I started to walk away, but when I heard Sandra on the phone again, I slowed my pace. "Hey, he just called," she sang into the phone with glee. "Well, he's definitely interested." I stopped dead in my tracks. To hell with pretending I wasn't listening. "I just have a feeling that this is it," she said. "He's the one, I can tell. He wants it bad." I couldn't bear to hear more. I made it back to my desk in record time, and also without my true emotions being detected on my face.

As I rounded my desk, my office line was ringing. "Blare, this is Garcelle." And, as though Satan himself were orchestrating my day, on the caller ID was the main number in Jacksonville.

"Good morning." Cortez's voice melted like butter on my

lightly toasted eardrum, but the silence that followed was violently loud. "You there?"

"Yes." I cleared my throat. "I'm here." I was speechless. All of the words I had for him seconds ago were pinned to the inside of my mouth. "Is there something you need me to do?" My regular, everyday words to him surfaced.

"Well . . ." He didn't sound happy. "To begin with, how are you?" he asked.

"I'm fine." I didn't know where the conversation was going. I didn't know who had the right to be more upset at the other. "If you're calling about that daily sales analogy report, I saw the error on page two, and will correct it and resend it before the meeting this afternoon."

"Not calling about the error. I haven't even opened the report or even my e-mail for that matter." It sounded like a door closed. "You wanna tell me what the hell happened to you on Friday night?"

"Nothing," I said nonchalantly. "What do you mean?"

"I came out of the bathroom and you were gone," he said. "And I never heard back from you."

"Oh, I'm sorry, I thought we were calling it a night." I paused. "I was drunk. I tried to call you, but it kept going to your voice mail," I lied, and rushed on. "How was the rest of your stay?"

"Garcelle, you should not have been driving that night, which is one reason I asked you to come up—"

"Oh, that's why you invited me up?" I said under my breath, but he didn't hear me.

"I was only in the bathroom for three or four minutes. You could've hung around a little longer." He took a deep breath and exhaled. "But, since you asked, my trip was nice."

I continued the conversation with as few feelings as I could pretend to have. "How about your luggage?" I asked. "Did you get it?"

"Yeah, early Saturday, but wait." He stopped himself, and I imagined him shaking his head. "Let me make sure I get this straight. When you left the room, you didn't leave angry or anything?"

"Angry? At what?" My façade was made of steel. "I guess I should've warned you about me drinking; I do crazy things like that."

"Damn!" He relaxed a tad. "Man, you had me worried. At first, I thought it was something I did or said, or didn't do or say." He added, "And then, as the time went by, I just worried about you getting to where you needed to be safely."

"Aw!" I rolled my eyes. "You were the perfect gentleman."

"Well, you haven't been very ladylike," he scolded me. "When a lady receives a call, she should pick up the phone." He turned the tables. "And I didn't get to this age by being stupid."

"Huh?" I was stumped.

"Come on, we had plans to go out the next night and all," he said. "So, how long are you going to pretend that the way things went down didn't bother you?"

I sat down in my chair, and used the moments of silence to decide what would be the best thing to say. The problem had now multiplied into something I wasn't even supposed to know about: Sandra. "Okay." I went back to the basics. "No one likes to be rejected."

"Rejected?" he interrupted me. "Who was rejected?"

"Look." I tried to keep my voice down. "We don't have to talk about it, it's done. We can just pretend that Friday never happened, and never bring it up again." I was serious, because I didn't want a weird cloud hovering over me professionally. He and Sandra could do what grown people do and never have to worry about having me stir anything up. "It's okay."

"No, it's not. What makes you think that I was rejecting you?" he asked.

"Well," I reminded him, "you kinda said it."

"No, I didn't." He straightened me out. "What exactly did I say?"

I whispered, "You said that you thought you had given me the wrong impression, and that you were not interested in having sex with me."

"Now, what part of that was rejection?" he asked.

Hello, McFly! "Is that a trick question?" I laughed. "You said that you had given me the wrong impression and that you weren't interested in me."

"I said that I wasn't interested in having *sex* with you," he corrected me. "You had gotten the wrong impression if you thought that I just wanted to have sex with you, and that's because I wanted so much more from you," he said. "I won't lie. If we lived in the same city, then I would've been on you like ketchup, because then I would still have the daily opportunities to see you and get to know you. But, because I knew our time was limited, I wanted to build on those simple things like your smile, scent, and touch." He brought his voice down. "Come on, sex I can get anywhere. Chemistry, I cannot, and that is what we have. We had it even before I got to Chicago. Would you say?"

"Yes," I confessed.

"Well," he spoke passionately, "I've done it wrong enough times to know when and how to do it right." He made perfect sense, and I believed him. I felt like a complete moron for allowing my insecurities to bombard a perfectly good evening. I thought back to the night, and remembered how my weight was a factor because I made it a factor. It's amazing the tricks the mind can play when you allow your weaknesses to have a voice.

"Well, I'm sorry for putting us in that situation to begin with," I said. "I shouldn't have approached you like that."

"Please approach me like that again," he joked. "This time, there won't be any morals, respect, or chemistry, just sweaty-butt-bootynaked sex." He chuckled.

"You don't mean that." I laughed.

"I do," he said. "It was hard as hell being good around you, and then you just leave a brother hanging. I was like damn, I should've just gone on and hit that, just kidding." He laughed. "I'm just kidding." Then he remembered. "And the funniest thing happened. I was thinking of you the next day at the wedding, just hoping you were okay, and at the reception, I start talking with this guy who selling an almost new saxophone, and his wife, Sandra, works with you at the Chicago office."

"Wow." I had an adrenaline rush and a smile. "Small world."

"Yeah, very," he said. "She's supposed to call me this evening to give me the final word. Her brother wants it, but doesn't want to pay for it, and they need the extra money. So I would say that it's mine," he said. "At least I hope."

"Okay." I put two and two together and knew what his talk with Sandra was about. I relaxed. "So, you play the sax?"

"Yeah," he answered lightheartedly. "I used to be in a band, but when I took this position here, I started missing gigs and they voted me out."

"Okay, so now you need to release an underground track dissin' them." I laughed. I couldn't believe how, in less than fifteen minutes, I had gone from wanting his head in the guillotine to wanting his arms around me again.

"Oh, wow! I didn't see the time," he grumbled. "I have a conference call about to start."

"Okay." I woke up from my dream. "I'll talk to you later then."

"No, wait." He got my attention. "What are you doing this evening?"

"Nothing." I quickly became excited, but remembered that he wasn't in my city. "Why?"

"I'll text you in an hour or so." He had to rush. "Okay?"

"Okay."

An hour later, I received the following text message from Cortez: *Let's cook tonight! Grocery list: Chicken breasts, long grain*

rice, block of mild cheese, broccoli, and a nice bottle of white wine.
Can you handle that?

Handled. I texted back on top of the world, and, as soon as I did, Jason appeared out of nowhere.

"What's up, gorgeous?" He smiled.

"Hi, Jason," I said, looking at him and wondering why God would play such a cruel joke by making him so damn handsome, yet so trifling. "What's going on?"

"Nothing much." He looked at me as though he could just lick me right then and there. Flashes of his member came to mind, and I had to catch my breath. "I was wondering when we were going to hang out again."

Just for kicks, I asked, "You came across a few dollars?"

"Nah." He patted his pockets. "Had some money on Friday, but I'm dead broke now, man."

I wanted to say, "Then why the fuck is your broke ass in my office asking me out again?" Instead, I just gave him a pitiful stare. "Yeah, I'm busted, too," I lied.

"Yeah." He shook his head. "Times are hard for everyone, man."

"So, what brings you in here today?" I asked.

"You!" He didn't hesitate with his answer, and smiled down at me. "I don't think you know, man." He blushed and glanced away shyly.

"Know what?" I was confused. "You don't think I know what?"

"How absolutely beautiful you are," he said, unable to look me in the face. "You're gorgeous, Garcelle."

I became warm inside. Even if the compliment was from the handsomest broke guy alive, it still meant a lot. "Thank you, Jason, that was sweet."

"That was real," he said. "I wish I had the money to really take you out." He shook his head. "But it's like there's always something with my money situation."

"I understand," I said.

"Well . . ." He glanced down at his zipper. "There are things that I can do for you that won't cost either of us a dime."

"Really?" I would've been offended if I didn't know just how big his dick was. "And what's that?"

"Well." He cleared his throat and moved closer to me in his baggy jeans. "I have this nagging suspicion that your pussy tastes like a peach, and I want to get to the bottom of it."

"A peach, huh?" I swallowed hard. "Why not strawberries or passion fruit?"

"Well, peaches are my favorite fruit. I can eat 'em for hours and not get tired." He continued in a whisper, "I already know that you're delicious. I can see it in the way you walk. I would split your juicy fruit open and suck on you all day." He added, "And it wouldn't cost you a thing."

"Jason," Ms. Jackson, his immediate supervisor, scolded him from down the hall. "We need you over here."

"Think about it." He winked at me. "I'll holla!"

I took a deep breath and tried hard not to think about his proposition. Lord knew that I needed one knocked out of the park for me, and Jason had the equipment to get the job done. I dedicated the next five minutes of company time imagining how Jason's tongue might feel licking and sucking on my clit and pussy lips. He was broke, tatted up, and living in his momma's basement, but there was something about his thug mentality and street swag that told me that pussy eating just could be his strong suit.

On the way home, I talked to Stacy on the phone and caught her up on everything: Cortez, Jason, and Stunna. "I like your nerve. How do you go from having no man to two and a half in a week?"

"Who in the hell is a half?" I asked, laughing.

"The one on that damn computer game." She referred to *Second Life*.

I gasped. "Stunna is a *great* guy. Why did you say that?"

"He's an avatar, Garcelle, another perfect-looking character in *Second Life* with flawless brown skin, a six-pack, perfectly cropped hair, and shiny bling." She laughed. "He might be a redneck in real life."

"You're an idiot." I giggled. "Nah, Stunna is black. We've talked on voice chat." I had to add, "He's your average Joe in Tennessee. He was laid off a couple months ago."

"And now he can't get off that game, so he'll stay laid off because he's not looking for a job. Whenever you log on, I bet his li'l laid, off tail is right there."

"Well, he works as a DJ in *Second Life*, so he makes money there and cashes it out into his Paypal account once a month." I tried to defend my virtual guy.

"Uh-huh. Hang that shit up, please, it sounds crazy," she said. "Just go to the grocery store and get the things Cortez suggested. I like him."

"And what about Jason?" I asked, already expecting the worst.

"Do I really need to advise you on Jason?" she asked.

"Duh," I joked. "Yes."

"I'd say make him your toy," she said.

"Toy?" I repeated for clarification.

"You know how you go to a concert to also enjoy the buildup of the opening acts? Well, big-dick men don't have opening acts." She laughed. "The big dick is the show." She went on, "In other words, you can't expect a big-dick dude to write you poetry and make breakfast in bed. He has a big dick, that's what he does."

"So, what are you saying?" I needed an answer.

"Use the big dick, don't let the big dick use you," she schooled me. "No more paying for drinks or anything of that nature, and don't feel sorry for his situation. If he can't at least meet you halfway financially, then he can't do a damn thing *but* give you that dick, so let him. Just don't let your feelings get involved. Treat him like a living, breathing dildo, that's it, that's all."

"That's so cold," I commented.

"You have to be cold when you don't wanna get hurt, Garci," she preached. "But we'll have to finish this up later. Our bowling league meets tonight and I have to get in the shower."

"Okay," I said.

"Let me know how your telephone dinner date goes." She giggled. "That's very cute, buying the same food items and on the phone cooking it together and eating it by candlelight two thousand miles apart," she teased. "That cell phone battery is going to burn the shit out of you."

"You are too silly." I cracked up. "Talk to you later."

I rushed into Jewel and grabbed the things Cortez asked me to get, stuff I needed for my diet, and a million things I didn't need. I got home and listened to my messages, then took a hot shower. At seven he called. We were both starving, so we wasted no time getting started. Simultaneously, we grilled our chicken breasts, cooked the rice, and steamed the broccoli florets, giving each other tips along the way. We sipped our wine and had conversation in between. It was different, and it felt like he was right there behind me at the stove. When the time came, we ended by adding grated cheese to the steaming hot rice, stirring in the broccoli, cubing the chicken, and mixing that in too. It was good, but I would've preferred to eat the food separately, not jumbled together.

I sat at my dining room table with him on the phone. At some point, we both had to switch to our home phones, because our cell phone batteries just couldn't handle our chat. We rudely ate in each other's ears, and ended up watching the same show on TV. We talked until after one in the morning.

The week went by super fast, and, like two giddy teenagers, Cortez and I talked late into the night every night. The night before, I started my no-meat-for-two-weeks diet. Cortez talked me into cooking and eating a T-bone steak, and I was so glad I did, it was amazing.

The first day I went without meat, fish, bread, and pop, and I thought I would die. It was like meat and Pepsi were walking around the office taunting me, but I stuck to it, and, the next morning, when I realized that I had gone twenty-four hours without meat or a Pepsi, I knew that I could go two weeks. So, each day, I would pack a large Ziploc bag of fruits, vegetables, yogurt, granola bars, and other healthy snacks, and carry it to work with me. I ate every three hours. At night, I would have a grilled veggie burger patty, brown rice, and a small salad. I was also doing aerobics for forty-five minutes each night from an exercise DVD. After a week, I was ready to claw everyone's faces off in the break room when I saw them eating, but I just dipped my baby carrots in my ranch dressing and kept on truckin'.

"Yay!" I said as I woke up the morning after the last day of my diet. I called Stacy. "Where's my scale?"

"In the sofa bed, open it up," she said. "I have to run, it's busy here."

I quickly replied, "Okay!"

"Text me the number of pounds lost," she said.

"I will." When I first started my diet, she came over, took my blood pressure, and did a few other things to ensure that I was in okay condition to start an exercise regimen. While she was there, I asked her to hide my scale so that I wouldn't go crazy weighing myself every six minutes.

I located my scale, and was nervous about stepping on it. What if I hadn't lost anything? What if I had gained somehow? No diet had ever worked for me. Well, maybe that was because I would always stop a day or two into it or modified it to my liking. So, this was the first time I had gone all out with diet and exercise.

I got buck-naked and hopped on the scale. I already knew

that if I didn't lose at least five pounds, I was going to eat a record book-size slice of cheesecake while still standing on the damn scale. I looked down at the numbers, and, at first, thought that it couldn't be right. I stepped off and stepped back on. It read 204; I had lost fifteen pounds. The way I screamed, my neighbors probably thought I had won the lottery. I ran straight to my cell phone and texted Stacy the news.

It was Friday and I felt like I was walking on air now. I grabbed a pair of size sixteen jeans that I had written off and tried my luck . . . they fit! Okay, maybe the word "fit" was a stretch. They were tight, and, once zipped up, I felt like I needed an oxygen mask, but they looked damn good to the untrained eye. Right as I opened my apartment door to leave, there was a floral deliveryman walking up with an arrangement. "Garcelle Monroe?" he asked.

"Yes." I was baffled. "What's this?"

"Flowers," he replied, as if he really thought I needed an answer.

I signed the paper and took the flowers. "Thank you," I said.

"Enjoy them," he replied and walked away.

I rested the flowers on the table, and I wrestled with the tiny envelope until I got the card out. It read: Happy Meat Day! Congratulations! Cortez.

"Oh, wow!" I said, covering my mouth with my hand. "My favorite, he remembered." During dinner at the hotel, I told him that yellow lilies were my favorite flower. "This is beautiful." I smiled. I stepped back from the arrangement to admire the yellow lilies, salal, pink roses, snapdragons, daisy poms, monte cassinos, pink carnations, and button poms. I grabbed my cell phone and dialed his number as I headed out the door. I got no answer, but was too excited to leave a message.

It was the middle of January, but inside I was as warm as a summer's day. I hadn't been able to reach Cortez, so a part of me wished the flowers would've been delivered to me at work. I wanted to stare at them and smile, and also be the envy of the office for a day. "Garcelle." Rachel, the main administrative assistant pranced into my office. "Bill wants to know if you will take this downtown." She dropped a binder, MapQuest directions, and a sealed envelope. "He said if you do it, you can have the rest of the day off." She pointed at the envelope. "Inside the envelope is one hundred dollars. That's for gas, parking, and lunch while you're down there."

I had made up my mind. "Tell Bill I'll see him on Monday." I smiled.

"Thank you," Rachel said. "Have a good weekend."

"I will," I said, and, before Rachel could get back to her desk, all of my things were packed up and I was locking up. "Have a good weekend, guys," I said to all in my area.

Heading downtown, I looked at the address. I knew the area where I was going, but didn't know exactly which building. I tried calling Cortez while I was in traffic, but there was still no answer. This time though, I left a message. "Hello, Mr. Yellow Lillies. I see that you were taking notes." I blushed. "The flowers are absolutely beautiful." Beautiful was an understatement. "You're an amazing man." I was thinking it, but wasn't supposed to speak it. "I'm off work already, so call me whenever you have a moment." I looked over at my car's clock. "It's a little after noon and I normally would have heard from you by now, so let me know that you're okay. Talk to you soon."

I pulled up in front of the address and saw a valet parking sign; it was a restaurant. *Oh, shit, who am I supposed to ask for in here?* I asked myself, but before I could grab my phone, the man was opening my door. "Thank you," I said, bringing my purse and the binder along. I walked through the front door and the hostess greeted me. "Welcome to Fogo de Chão."

"Hi." I looked around for anyone that looked like they were

waiting for someone or something. "I'm supposed to be meeting someone here to give them something from my company."

"Oh." Something rang a bell to her. "From Blare Corp?" she read from her sheet.

"Yes, that's me," I answered.

"Okay, one moment please." She called another girl over and explained to her where to take me.

I followed the other hostess to the table, but no one was there. She said, "I see his drink is still here, so he may be in the restroom." She pulled out a chair. "Have a seat."

I sat there for a full two minutes before I realized that the centerpiece on the table consisted of yellow lilies. For a split second, I romanced myself with the thought that they were for me, which made my nightly conversations with Cortez replay in my head. As I impatiently tapped on the binder, I looked around the restaurant for more yellow lilies and saw none. I glanced back at the ones right in front of me, and, right on cue, I heard his voice in my ear. "May I join you?" Cortez asked from behind me, taking the Blare binder out of my hand.

"Oh my God!" I mouthed to myself and sprung to my feet. "Oh my God! Are you serious?" He was supposed to be in Jacksonville, not Chicago. I turned to face him, and knew I wouldn't be able to look away for a while. My hands wrapped around his neck, as his found their place around my waist. Our lips met for a quick, we-are-in-public peck. I wanted so much more, but I promised myself that I would let him steer us in the direction we would go. "What are you doing here?" I asked excitedly.

"Here to take a friend to lunch," he said.

"Oh my God." My hands covered my mouth. "You came all the way here to take a friend to lunch?"

"Yeah, she's been starving herself, not eating meat, fish, bread." He then joked, "She was on some crazy diet, but it's over today, so she can eat meat now . . . right?" He looked at me for an answer.

"Yes, but I'm still gonna go easy on the meat," I informed him.

"No comment." He laughed. "But, for the record, going easy on the meat is no fun."

"What?" I thought back to what I said. "Oh, my goodness, you know what I mean."

Cortez looked me up and down hungrily. "You look great and feel even better." He pulled me in, and wrapped his hands around my waist again, and I felt heaven in his touch. Thank God we had a corner table, because this time I couldn't help but hold him; it felt natural. Gazing into each other's eyes, the general consensus was to not be a public spectacle, but we couldn't fight the feeling. Right there, as though no one else were around, our lips said hello and didn't know how to say good-bye in English, so we kept them together to explore passion in whatever language they spoke.

It felt like we were kissing for a record-breaking amount of time, but, in actuality, I knew the instrumental song playing, and our lips touched right at the beginning of it and it hadn't even made it to the first chorus yet. We pecked at each other a few times before sitting in our respective seats next to, and not across from, each other.

"Wow, you're here. This is insane." I adjusted my legs. "What are you doing here?" I asked again out of the pure shock that I was in.

"I'm very proud of you," he said. "You've been dieting, and had to deal with me eating chicken, ribs, drinking fish grease, and snacking on cookies in your ear on the phone while you were having salads, veggie burger patties, and rabbit food," Cortez joked. "This is the least I can do."

"Wow!" I was flabbergasted. "You didn't have to come all the way here. We could've cooked and eaten on the phone tonight."

"Damn!" he exclaimed. "Sounds like you don't want to see me."

"Oh, no," I corrected him. "That couldn't be further from the truth."

"Good," he said. "Let me leave the corny shit alone and just tell you that I just needed to see you." He touched my face. "All the talking we have done has truly piqued my interest."

"Wow." I gulped.

He looked uncomfortable. "Man, you got a brother feeling a little self-conscious about dropping in," he said. "Did you have plans this afternoon or something?"

"No," I said. "Honestly, I'm just a little lost for words."

He asked, "In a good way, I presume?"

"In a great way," I answered. "Oh, and thank you for the beautiful flowers. I've been calling you since this morning."

"I know." He smiled. "I was at the airport and I'm not a very good liar. I would've said something to give myself away, so I just couldn't answer my phone, sorry."

"No problem." I was looking at him as if I were staring at a ghost. "I can't believe that you came all the way here for me."

"You don't think you're worth it?" he asked.

"Oh, of course I am," I told him. "I'm worth flying to the moon for."

"Fly me to the moon. Let me play among the stars." He tried his best at Sinatra. "Let me see what spring is like on Jupiter and Mars."

"Very good." I was impressed. "I didn't know that you could sing."

"I have to keep some things to myself. That's my way of making you come back for more," he said.

"Keep it coming then." I smiled.

"You hungry?" he asked.

"Extremely," I answered.

Fogo de Chão was an authentic Brazilian steakhouse. The ambience was warm, with white linen tablecloths, live flowers, candles, and soft music whispering from above. The gourmet salad bar was extensive. The waitress brought the endless sides, which were warm cheese bread, crispy hot polenta, gar-lic mashed potatoes, and caramelized bananas. You are given a round card that is red on one side and green on the other. You turn your card green side up, signaling that you are ready for the gaucho chefs to begin carving and serving your meat tableside. And as long as your card is green side up, they will keep visiting your table to bring you more and more meat. I'm talking sirloin, filet mignon, rib eye, beef ribs, lamb, chicken, pork ribs, and sausage.

I felt the threads on my jeans giving way one by one and threatening to embarrass me, so I finally flipped my card to red. I probably had every type of meat there was. The service was great and the food was even better. I also had a drink, my first alcoholic beverage in two weeks. Cortez and I ate, drank, and talked, and then talked, talked, and talked. When we left the restaurant, it was almost four.

"Where to?" I asked after the valet driver brought the car up.

"Um." He thought for a while. "The building that you were supposed to take me to."

"Oh, the Hancock Building," I said. "We can go up to the ninety-sixth floor where the bar is and take in the view, it's fabulous." I loved going up there.

At the Hancock, we parked and made our way to the eleva-tors. Since it was still midday, there was no line, and we were able to get a table by the window.

I marveled as I towered over the Chicago skyline. "This is amazing, isn't it?"

"Yes, this is pretty awesome," he said, as he looked down in awe.

"You know," I pointed out, "you can see four states from up here: Illinois, of course; Wisconsin; Indiana; and Michigan."

"I'm sure that's true and all," he said, "but I see something even more amazing not even two feet away from me."

"Do you?" I blushed. "And what might that be?"

"The drink menu." He had a great sense of humor. "I need a drink if I'm going to be this high up." He laughed. "Of course, I meant you, but I'm sure I have told you enough today just how great you are in every aspect; I don't want to overdo it." He pulled my chair out.

We sat down, and Cortez ordered a bottle of champagne. It was served in a gorgeous sterling silver bucket filled with ice, accompanied by two champagne flutes garnished with a strawberry inside each. He poured the champagne, and then put pressure on me to come up with a toast. "Well, instead of toasting, how about we make wishes?"

"Sounds fun," he said. "What's yours?"

"Hold up, nosey," I slowed him down. "It doesn't work like that."

"School me then," he said suggestively.

"Oh, I *will* school you." I looked at how his chest sat up so chiseled in his shirt. "I say we write down three wishes each and exchange them, but we can only open one each time we spot another couple kissing."

"Deal." He agreed to my corny game. "You have paper?"

"I should," I said. I looked through my purse and found some pink Post-it notes . . . that had to have fallen out of my filing cabinet into my purse, because I would never steal office supplies . . . right? "Here you go." I gave him three.

For about five minutes, we pondered our wishes, wrote them down, and then exchanged the papers. We were thirty minutes into a completely new conversation when he pointed at something behind me. "Wish time," he said. I turned to see an elderly couple holding hands and pecking on the lips. He opened up one of the notes and read it loudly. "'I wish I would've met you five years ago.'" He paused. "Why do you wish that?"

I started bragging. "I told you how bad my body used to be back in the day," I said. "I would love to look like that now."

"Well, we all were in better shape years ago, but how would it make any difference in who you are today?" he asked.

Oh, God, this is where all of my insecurities could be brought to the light. "I guess it wouldn't change me from being who I am, but I would be a little more confident and more open to do certain things."

"Things like what?" he asked.

I was setting myself up to sound like a real loser. "Wearing a two-piece bikini, for one, so you won't be getting me out on the beach," I said.

"Listen," he said to get my attention. "There's nothing wrong with you, so you need to walk around with more confidence in yourself." He charmed me. "I'm sitting here in front of what has to be the best view of Chicago in the whole damn city, and yet I cannot stop looking at you." He went on. "I think you're incredibly beautiful, and I support what you're trying to do with your weight for your health, but I personally wouldn't change a thing about you."

"Thank you," I said, touching his arm. When I had first started my diet, I told him that my doctor suggested that I lose weight. Doctor's orders were always a great statement to use, because then people wouldn't hit you with the sympathy "you don't need to lose weight" speech to try to not offend you by agreeing that you could shed a few pounds.

"If you don't believe me, then read this." He pulled out one of his wishes that I should read first. "Read it."

"Let's see here." I unfolded the paper and held it close enough for me to read his small handwriting. "'I wish to be making love to you before midnight.' Don't be so shy," I said sarcastically.

"It's just a wish," he said. "No pressure. All wishes don't come true."

"I know," I said. But if I had anything to do with it, his wish would be reality at quarter to nine.

"Just please don't run out on me this time," he begged. "I'm scared to go to the restroom." He chuckled.

I drew an x over my heart with my index finger. "I promise."

"Thanks." He winked. "Because I would hate to have to resort to using handcuffs to keep you near me."

My eyebrows lifted. "Handcuffs?" I asked.

"Yep," he said. "The real kind."

"Mm." I smiled. "I can dig it."

"Really?" he flirted. "I can dig you."

I spotted a couple sitting by the piano, smooching. "Oh, look." I pointed and then snatched up one of his wishes. "Kissers over there." I unfolded his paper and read it aloud. "'I wish I could have one last conversation with my father,'" his words read. *Lord! Who told him to get all sentimental?* This wasn't the time for a mournful exchange, not while we were drinking and a mile up in the sky. However, because it was obviously something that was on his mind, I asked, "What would you say to your dad?"

"Actually, I would just want to listen to what he would say to me," he said. "I would love to soak up his wisdom. Just a fraction of what he knew would make me ten times the man I am." He shook his head from side to side. "I would love to hear his voice, it wouldn't even matter what he had to say."

I didn't know how deep into talking about his dad he wanted to get, so I simply asked, "How old were you when he passed away?"

"I was seventeen," he recalled. "A senior in high school."

I grimaced, and commented, "Wow, that must've been tough."

"Tough isn't the word," he said, grabbing for my next wish. He unfolded it and read it. "'I wish that you lived here and we were able to do these things all the time.'" I blushed as he read my words. "Yeah, that would be nice," he agreed. "That would be real nice."

Right then, Colbie Caillat's "Bubbly" played softly through the speakers. "Oh, my goodness, I love this song. I haven't heard it in a while, though."

"Wanna dance?" he asked.

I giggled. "Yeah, if there were a dance floor here."

"We don't need one," he said, reaching for my hand. "Let's make our own." He pulled me out of my chair.

"Are you serious?" I asked.

"Yes," he said. "Sometimes, you just have to do what you want to do, and to hell with not being in the right place to do it. You may never make it to wherever the right place is." He pulled me close. "Let's dance."

At first, I felt foolish dancing without a dance floor or anyone else in the room dancing, but before Colbie really started to "bubble," I was nestled against him as if my life depended on it. The feeling she described in the song was the way Cortez made me feel. "It starts in my toes/ make me crinkle my nose/where ever it goes I always know."

After the dance, I turned and put my back on his chest. I was facing the window, admiring the awesome view. "Thank you for making me do that," I said over my shoulder.

"What, dance?" he asked.

"Yes," I said. "I would've never thought of doing it or had the guts to."

"There's nothing to it." He rubbed my shoulders. "You have to seize your own moments or you won't have any moments, to talk about."

"That's true," I said. "Well, thank you."

"No." He kissed my earlobe. "Thank you." Cortez turned me to the side, and his lips caught the corner of mine. I turned so that I could give them to him fully. "Looks like we're on to the third wish," he said.

"Who?" I looked around to find the couple he was referring to. "I don't see anyone."

He tickled my sides. "You and me."

"Oh!" I laughed.

"Okay." I picked up the last piece of paper. I was eager to read it. "'I wished you lived in Jacksonville.'" I blushed, and didn't feel so bad about my earlier wish. However, the wish of mine he was about to read was something I shouldn't have owned up to. I actually didn't expect us to go through with these wishes; I just wanted to get out of the toast. I thought for sure we would've been caught up and not given it a second thought.

"Drum roll please," he said, as he unfolded the last torn piece of paper. "'I wish I already knew how big you were, so that I could stop obsessing about it.'" He chuckled. "Whoa."

"I never in a million years thought that we would actually remember to read these wishes," I said, blushing. "Oh my God!"

"Listen, let's get out of here," he said while caressing my back. "Let me put your mind to rest."

"You wanna ease my mind?" I flirted and raised my eyebrows.

"Yeah, I'll ease your mind." He then whispered directly into my ear, "I wanna ease a lot of things on your body."

"Mm." I rubbed his chest. "Are you in the easing business?"

"I'm in the pleasing business, girl." He nibbled on my ear. "I want you to be a little hungry for me, so that I can ease and please you."

I playfully bit his cheek. "Is this hungry enough?"

He smiled. "Put on your coat, and let's go find out." He waved the server over, and, in minutes, we were waiting in a long line to get onto the elevator. We zoomed out of the garage. Strangely, there wasn't much traffic, giving me less time to think of creative ways to hide my stomach if things really got on and poppin'.

Back at the hotel, the minute we hung up our coats, he pinned me up against the wall. He looked me in my eyes and reminded me, "There will be no running away tonight." His chest smashed into my heaving cleavage, as his lips inched in closer to mine. He took control of the kiss, and made it even more passionate than I expected. His hands traveled down the sides of my body until they were both resting on my sides. He then lifted me away from the wall so that he could get a feel of my behind.

With lips still locked, he backed himself into the opposite wall of the corridor, so I became the aggressor. I pulled his tongue into my mouth and playfully sucked on it, sending his imagination running wild on what else I could suck on to make his toes curl. I rubbed his chest ravenously, and I explored his mouth with the same fire-hot intensity. "So," I repeated the question from earlier, "is this hungry enough?"

He ran his fingers through my hair. "No, I want you mouth-watering hungry."

"You have something that will make my mouth water?" I asked seductively.

"Oh, do I." He smirked. "I have something that will make your mouth do all sorts of things."

"Is that so?" I nibbled on his bottom lip.

He reached for my hand and rested it on the front of his pants. I went in for the squeeze-and-rub test to determine if he had something worth my while, or if I had another Mitch on my hands. From the feel of it, it was very thick. I couldn't tell the exact length, but the circumference was impressive. "Does that make your mouth water?" he asked.

"Um." I pretended to think. "No, not yet." I continued to rub him. "Maybe a full presentation might help."

"I can make that happen." He undid his belt and zipper, and pushed his pants toward the floor, when suddenly out of the peephole of his silk boxers sprung the head of a caramel delight. Our lips met again, and I couldn't help stroking his solid, thick eight inches.

"Mm," I found myself moaning as I fondled him below.

"Yeah," he groaned, and stepped completely out of his pants. "Mm." I tightened my grip on his fat shaft, and softly squeezed him to the tip of his meat several times, watching his eyes flutter in ecstasy on each stroke. "Oh, shit," he said, biting into his lips. "Whew!"

"Is this hungry enough?" I playfully asked, as I jerked him off and licked his lips.

"I'd have to put it in your mouth to see how hungry you really are," he said. "You down for that?"

"I might be." I batted my eyes like a good girl and said, "Let's see."

As he walked over to the bed, I made it my personal duty to turn off the lights in the room along the way. Only the bathroom light needed to be on, plus it provided enough of a glow for us to see each other. When I made it to the bed, he was coming out of his T-shirt, and was completely naked before me.

"Get comfortable," he said while lying back onto his elbows. "Get naked."

I would've much rather he take off my clothes than for him to lie back and watch. I felt like a spectacle, but I slowly pulled down my jeans, and, after stepping out of them, I unbuttoned several of the buttons on my brown top and exposed my lacey beige bra. "Take it off," he instructed, as his hand caressed his piece slowly.

Taking off my shirt wasn't in the plan as yet. I wanted to first impress him with my "little gag reflex" tricks before he saw more of my body, so I approached the bed anyway. "Take your shirt off." I rolled my eyes in the dim lighting and granted his wish, revealing one of my only matching bra-and-panties sets. "Very nice." He smiled. "Come put this in your mouth and show me just how hungry you are."

I knelt on the floor before him as though to worship his dick, an idol god. I stroked him up and down several times before wiping my moist, warm tongue up the length of his muscle, and flicked my tongue wildly over and around his dome tip. I covered his head with wet tongue kisses and then dropped my mouth down over it, gliding down as if it was greased.

"Damn!" he shrieked.

I loved sucking dick. It was one of those things that you know that you're good at, so you just sit back and watch people marvel at your talent . . . that was me with a dick in my mouth, simply marvelous. I moisturized him with saliva, then wrapped my lips around his meat, swallowing him as if I was a backsliding vegetarian. His hefty hive in my mouth made my honeycomb drip sweetness into my panties. As I sucked him down, I stroked his big beef upward and took all of his delectable flavors into my taste buds. After ten minutes of my lips and tongue tantalizing his buzzing hive, his hot honey erupted into my mouth.

He stood up and flipped me onto my back, and his tongue dove down between my thighs as if it were attached to a rocket. He held the lips of my dripping wet peach open with his fingers, then gently sucked on my pearl of flesh, as though it were truly a gem that was attached to my body. He rubbed it with his fingers, licked it, and then inserted his two fingers as he stroked it with his tongue. My oil tanker exploded, and, soon, there was an outpouring of creamy oil coating my fruit and his lips.

"Damn," he mumbled, "I have to feel you." He disappeared into the bathroom and came back with a condom on. On his way back to the bed, he turned on the light next to the bed. I gasped, but had no time to truly react, because he was already between my legs, spreading them, about to give me the business. His hardness parted my lips and fought to get through. Cortez pushed and pushed and finally fell into my tight spot. "Shit, girl," he uttered.

"Mm," I moaned in ecstasy. "Yes." I exhaled. It had been a long time, and I was relishing the moment. "Oh, God, yes!"

"You feel amazing," he said, pushing into me over and over again. "Damn." He was already starting to sweat. The heat from our bodies might have been enough to burn Chicago down again. He filled me to capacity and felt wonderful inside of me. After a few minutes, I was sure that the people next door wanted it to all be over so that my loud groaning and grunting would end. But Cortex rolled me onto my stomach and then I really acted like a fool.

"Oh my God!" I screamed. "Oh, yes."

"Yeah?" he asked. "You like that?"

"Yes, I do," I answered, half out of breath. "I love it."

"Mm, yeah." He pushed with more vigor. "Can you take it all?" he asked.

"Give it to me," I ordered.

With each thrust into me, he reached new depths that he hadn't the time before. He was tearing down walls in my pussy and I loved it. My eyes closed in pleasure, and then I felt them roll back in bliss. "I'm coming," I squeezed out just in time, and then my body spat pearls, and then collapsed.

"Oh, shit." I felt his body jerking and then he slammed into me one final time. "Oh, man!" his winded voice exclaimed. "Damn!" He then rolled off me and onto the bed.

I wrestled to get under the covers and away from the light. "Where are you going?" he asked.

"I'm a little cold," I lied. "I'm trying to get under the covers."

"Oh"—he lifted up so that I could get under—"come here." He pulled me close to him, and rubbed my arms and then my butt. "Got a little freak in you I see, huh?"

I blushed. "Doesn't everyone?" I asked.

"I can't speak for everyone, but I can raise my hand to be sure about you," Cortez said. "Damn, that was good."

"Did you expect something different?" I asked.

Right then, his phone rang. "I have to pick this call up." He reached over to the nightstand. "This is Cortez," he answered. "Yeah, I have the binder," he said. "No, not yet, I've been a little busier than I expected." He fought to control the conversation. "Look, Bill, let me call you back."

"Is everything okay?" I asked when he hung up the phone.

"Yeah," he said. "Bill is just a little too impatient at times, but everything is cool," he said. "You ready for round two?"

"Let's go." I was tired, but I had never turned down a doubleheader and wasn't about to start now.

He asked, "Wow, you are ready to go again?"

"We can wait if you don't have it together," I teased. "I didn't come here to break anything," I joked.

"Oh, it can't be broken," he said. "You can come ride it 'til the wheels fall off right now."

"Whoa, don't saddle up just yet, cowboy," I joked. "Gimmie a few."

"Oh, so you were just talking shit?" he said. "You can't back it up."

We both laughed as he pulled me closer. My eyes fell shut and I was in heaven. When I opened my eyes again, I was shocked to see that it was after 10:00, and, except for the numbers on the clock, the room was pitch black. I hated being in the dark, so I stretched out and rolled over to be by his side, but found that I was alone. "Cortez?" I called his name. "Hello?" I panicked in the darkness, and nearly knocked the night table's lamp over trying to turn it on. "Cortez?"

He didn't answer. I held my shirt up over my nakedness and walked around the room, but he wasn't there. I needed something to wear, so I hesitantly walked over to his suitcase to look for a T-shirt. I tussled through a few of his items and came across some financial documents from the company. I overlooked them when I ran into a T-shirt. I jumped into the shower and heard him enter the room as I lathered up. Though the door was open, he didn't disturb me, and I was grateful. As I moisturized, I smelled pepperoni pizza and nearly lost my mind. A minute later, I looked at my reflection with his T-shirt on, and, though it fit me snugly, it was kind of cute.

"Hey." He looked up from his suitcase at me. "You went through my bag?"

"Yeah." I was a little taken aback. "I needed something to put on."

"Oh!" He then noticed the shirt and cracked a smile. "It looks nice on you." Cortez pointed to the pizza box on the bed. "I hope you like pepperoni."

"I love pepperoni." I shook my head. "I can't stay around you too long or you'll make me gain every pound back."

"I'm having some drinks brought up," he said. "The Cavaliers are playing tonight."

"Okay," I said, wondering why he was so concerned about his suitcase. "I didn't steal anything," I joked, as I pointed at his suitcase.

"Funny!" He laughed. "Nah." He waved it off. "I just have some Blare confidential information with me, that's all." He walked over and put his hands around my waist.

"Oh." I shrugged my shoulders and lied, "I didn't see any papers." I tugged on the shirt I was wearing. "This was right on the top."

"No prob, Bob." He smacked my butt.

"Ouch." I playfully ran away from him and jumped in the bed.

Our drinks arrived, and the game was at halftime break when, on my third slice, Cortez pulled me closer to him and kissed my neck. "Sorry for spooking you out about my suitcase."

"No problem. Just as long as you don't have a gun or a dead body in there, then we're fine," I said.

"Nah." He chuckled. "Just those damn papers." He huffed lightheartedly. "Sometimes, I want to put *my* bank account number on one of those papers."

"Oh, put mine on there too," I joked. "Mama needs a new pair of shoes."

He rubbed my arm. "Man, if you only knew."

I asked, "If I only knew what?"

Why did I ask that question? Cortez completely ignored the game and spent the next hour discussing the strong financial stance of the company. He went on to say that new branches would be opening and great positions would be available everywhere. He then started telling me things I was sure I wasn't supposed to know about the inner workings of the company. He then joked, "Boy, you and I doing a few wrong things together could be dangerous."

"Ha! Ha! Ha!" I shook my head. "Don't get any bright ideas."

"I'm just being truthful," he said. "Let's just say—"

"No," I cut him off. "No, let's just *not* say."

"Hypothetically," he raised his voice. "This is all hypothetical." He paused for a moment to see if I would allow him to speak.

"Hypothetical conversations are a waste of time," I said, giggling, "but go on, speak your piece."

"Okay." He explained, "Every department reports their sales to you and you report to your management and the home office," he said. "So, let's say you skim a dollar off each department's total. You keep ten dollars for yourself and no one will know."

"That's stupid," I said. "Number one, you just said I report the numbers to manage in my office, too, plus I report the earnings, but I never see the actual money, so it would be a waste."

"Not if, say, you were working with someone in management who takes the money to the bank." Cortez's voice changed.

"You tell him to take ten dollars out of the bank deposit and you're good to go." He went on. "Y'all could split it seven three, you getting seven, of course."

"But the department heads would know that the numbers are wrong," I said, really thinking of a way to prove him wrong. "Can't be done."

"Oh." He rubbed my back. "Anything can be done."

"True, but that's if you want anything *to* be done," I said. "That's not me. I would never agree to anything like that." Remembering something my mom always said, "You never do wrong and get by" I laughed and moved my head from side to side. "Plus, I'm way too paranoid to roll with the big dogs like that, no, sir."

"So, if I had a way to put two or three thousand extra dollars a month in your pocket, you wouldn't hear me out?" he asked.

"What?" I snickered and looked over at him to see a serious expression on his face. "Are you serious?"

"Yes," he said. "Just let me explain."

He went on and on about how he and Bill went to college together. He was the one who got Bill hired as a manager. Apparently, they had already discussed this whole scam, but needed me, the missing link, to be a part of it. It was a well thought-out plan that had to have taken some time for him to sit and work out the logistics. I got an instant headache from his voice.

"Wait a minute." I had to know. "So all of this"—I pointed back and forth between the two of us—"was just to get me in on it?"

"No." He laughed. "Bill and I have only been talking about it for a day or two." He shifted. "I told him that I would run it by you, but if you weren't interested, we would scrap it."

I was feeling uneasy. "I feel used."

"Used?" He chuckled. "Nothing has even gone down."

"This has gone down." I pointed at the bed. "Was this get-rich-quick scheme your only interest all along?" I questioned.

"Relax," he said, and massaged my shoulders from behind. "I told you that we just started talking about it. It's truly no big deal." He kissed the side of my face. "Let's just forget it, okay?" He remembered something. "As a matter of fact, there should be a thousand dollars in that envelope Bill sent you with; it's for your trouble and your silence."

"What, and for my sex, too?" I scooted out of the bed. "Wow, this is so not what I expected from you."

"What?" He jumped up. "What we have and what I just talked to you about have nothing to do with each other."

"You expect me to believe that?" I asked. "You have been grooming me all this time."

"That hurts," he said. "That really hurts." He walked away. "I can't believe you can actually stand there and say that." He turned to face me. "The way you have made me feel over the last few weeks is amazing. Coming here and being with you like this is making me happier than I have been in a very long time." He shook his head. "No amount of money is worth this." He put his hand over his heart. "I swear this has nothing to do with the reason I want to be with you." He continued in a whisper, "I love you!"

"What?" I stopped dead in my tracks. "What?"

"Nothing!" he yelled, and walked into the bathroom and slammed the door.

I couldn't believe my ears. *Did he just say that he loved me?* I knew that I was falling for him, so it was possible, but I wasn't close to saying I love you, even though inside, I probably did. However, in the middle of this, was I supposed to believe that now? Was this even real? Regardless of what he said, I couldn't get over the feeling that asking me to go along with his evil plan was his only interest in me. And now look, I was caught with my panties down, literally. I started to put on my clothes when he came out of the restroom.

"Please don't leave," Cortez said, walking toward me. "I'm sorry if I made you feel a certain way."

"It's cool," I lied. "I just need time to swallow all of this."

"So, what are you saying?" he asked. "You'll think about it?"

"I might!" I lied, as I put on my coat. "I'll think about the money part, but the *us* part I don't know about." I shrugged my shoulders. "I just feel like I was the missing piece of your puzzle. You needed me, you didn't necessarily like me. It's just that without me changing the reports, you can't do any of this." I asked for confirmation. "Right?"

He couldn't answer. "Look." He stumbled over his words. "I liked you and wanted to get to know you before any of this came about."

"I don't know, Cortez." I grabbed my purse and the envelope. "This is all a little suspect right now." I wanted to get out of the room. Apparently, I didn't really know him, so I didn't know what he was capable of. "I need to think about all of this."

He then said, "Even if it doesn't work out between us, personally, I would still want you in on this. I know that you need the money."

"You and I have never discussed my finances," I huffed, "so how do you know what I need?" I got angry. "Don't try to sell me on this bullshit right now. I told you that I will think about it, don't push it."

"Fine." He put his hands up to signal surrender. "How about I call you in the morning?"

"I'll call you," I said, and took one last look at him.

He was very strategic in hiring Bill and whomever else he needed there to steal money from the company, and now I was in the middle of it. Sure, I could use the extra money; I could save up and get a house in Olympia Fields, a new car even. I was dreaming big, but what happened if we were caught? I wasn't built for prison; I have been a girly girl all my life. I had never been in a fistfight or even knew if I could land a punch. I would have to be some lesbian gangbanger's bitch minutes after I received an inmate number.

Cortez used his smoke and mirrors wisely, as any master illusionist should. He was a fraud who deceived me well. If this were all a magic act, he would get a standing ovation. The crowd would roar and the applause would resound for minutes after he left the stage.

As soon as I crawled into bed, my cell phone's ring tone played. It was after one in the morning, and the display showed Cortez's name. I put the phone back on the dresser, but an overwhelming urge made me grab it and answer. "Hello!" He didn't say anything. "Hello?" I called out again.

"Damn," I heard his voice faintly. "Oh, shit!"

I called his name again. "Cortez." It sounded like he was in pain, so I continued to pay attention.

"Mm," he cried. "You couldn't wait until we got to the room, huh? You had to get you some right here in the elevator?" He laughed. "That's why I can't get tired of you." I heard the smile in his voice. "Mm, yeah, suck that dick." He paused and groaned. "Suck it all." I was aghast, and sat up in bed when I heard the elevator bell ding. I listened as he walked to the room, and heard the lock beep as he used his keycard.

"Now, come get on this dick," he demanded. "Let me fuck that sweet man pussy."

"You love this tight little man cunt, don't you?" I recognized the voice of Bill, William Taylor, the manager from the office. "Oh!" he yelped. "Oh, yeah, fuck me, big daddy."

"No, you fuck me," Cortez said, followed by a loud smack. "Ride that cock." There was another smack. "Fuck me."

They painted such a vivid picture that I was sick to my stomach, yet I couldn't bring myself to hang up. For the next fifteen minutes, I could almost see Cortez stuffing Bill full of cock. At one point, they were going so hard that I could hear the slapping of Cortez's midsection against Bill's ass. There was grunting and groaning, and they topped off with Cortez sucking off Bill and taking a load in his mouth.

"This is not what we came here for," Cortez said in laughter.

Bill, breathing heavily, asked, "Isn't that what we always say?"

"Yeah," Cortez agreed with a chuckle. "Somehow we always end up this way before we get down to business."

"Well, it's a good thing," Bill interjected. "Now I can actually listen to what you have to say without sitting here wondering how long before I'm sucking that dick."

"Yeah, I know, and I would be thinking the same thing," Cortez said. "I still don't see how we finished senior year." He cleared his throat. "But on to business. I don't know if Garcelle is going to do it."

"Damn!" Bill said. "You told her that I was already in?"

Cortez said, "Yeah."

"Shit!" Bill interjected. "I told you that you—"

"Calm down," Cortez spoke over him. "I'll hear from her tomorrow. She was leaning, just not as far as I wanted her to lean. I got another angle I can work with her, but as a last resort, I got enough video of us fucking to change that." He laughed.

"You sneaky son of a bitch," Bill said, and I heard them slap palms. "How did you do that?"

"The camera was on top of the armoire, sticking out of my toiletry bag," Cortez bragged. "She never even questioned it."

Bill asked, "So, what's up with her?"

"She's supposed to call me in the morning," Cortez said, and continued in a growl, "Let me get some more of that man pussy."

"Take your pants completely off this time," Bill instructed. "That was too much work."

With the removal of his pants, he must've realized that his phone was on. "I hate this damn touch phone," Cortez said. "It was trying to call out." That was the last thing I heard, and that was all I needed to hear.

I couldn't believe my ears. He recorded us having sex so that he could force me to cooperate, or blackmail me, or whatever the hell he was planning to do, but this whole thing wasn't as simple as me saying I didn't want to do it. I didn't know what to do, but I didn't call him and I ignored all of his calls. Early Monday morning, I called work to say that I would not be coming in. Immediately after, I called the home office and spoke to the CEO's secretary. I told her that there were people trying to steal from the company and had asked me to help. I was too surprised when Mr. Faison's personal assistant returned my call, and asked if I could fly out to Jacksonville the next morning. It was an all expense–paid trip and I loved it! That was, until all of the corporate bigwigs and two FBI agents later met with me in a private conference room.

I told them everything, including the dick-on-dick listening session I attended. I even brought the hush money with me so that I was completely vindicated of this ordeal. They didn't want to just fire Cortez and Bill, they wanted to arrest them. Cortez was already under surveillance in a money-laundering investigation, and would've eventually been caught and we all would've gone down.

They had me call Cortez and agree to change the numbers. He was overjoyed. The information they wanted to know, Cortez happily and unknowingly provided them with, even details about me sexually as I cringed. Over a three-week pe-riod, Cortez had me change the numbers eight times. Alto-gether, $17,804 was taken, $3,000 of which was promised to me. The day we were all meeting at a restaurant to receive the cash is when it went down, zip-zam-zoom. Cortez, Bill, and two others from my company were all arrested. I was then off

from work with pay until the new location opened in Joliet in
six months, where I was promised a managerial position.

Five months later, it was close to summer and almost time
for me to return to work. I had relocated forty miles southwest
of Chicago to Joliet two months prior. I got up at 8:00 A.M.
five mornings a week and went to the gym, which included
three aerobics classes a week. When I got home, I'd wash up,
run some errands, shop, and get some me time in. I stopped
eating so many fried foods, cut meat out of my diet for a week
every month, and, during the other weeks, I tried to have no
more than seven ounces a meat a day. To date, I was down
forty-two pounds and I was feeling great.

Stacy was four months pregnant, and I loved hearing her
talk about the baby and the various childbirth milestones she
was approaching. I longed to have that experience someday.
I was helping two other nurses from her job plan a surprise
baby shower for her.

In the evenings, I was basically on the couch or in bed,
curled up with my laptop, playing *Second Life*. Stunna76 and
I finally exchanged real-life pictures via e-mail. He was a very
large man, and when I say large, from the looks of it, the fire
department might have to break down a wall or two to get
him out. I was floored because his avatar looked like a chocolate Adonis. I didn't trip though, because I didn't look like
the girl on the screen either, even with the weight I lost.

Stunna76's voice had me fooled though, because Lord
knows I beat my pussy up with a dildo many times as his character chained me to a dungeon wall and forced me to perform
sexual acts. Well, I can't lie. Once I knew what he looked
like, our sex life was over and done with, but we were still a
couple . . . until one of my sorority sisters copied me on her
chat log with Stunna76. Smoke and mirrors again, ladies and

gentlemen. Stunna76 was a pussy-hunting dog, and I paid the thirty-two dollars in game fees and divorced him, freeing my profile of his name and mine from his.

I was sitting at home in an Alpha Phi Kappa meeting on *Second Life* when my cell phone went off with a number I didn't recognize. I didn't answer, but the person called right back. I informed my sisters I would be off the microphone for a few minutes.

"Hello?" I said in the mouthpiece.

"Hi, Garcelle?" the gentleman asked cautiously.

I got nervous, because Cortez had called and threatened me from prison shortly after he received his eight-year sentence. "Who is this?"

"This is Jason," he said. "Is this still Garcelle's number?"

"Yeah." I relaxed. "Hi, Jason."

"Well, damn, secret service agent," he joked. "How you doing?"

I laughed. "I'm doing all right." I was genuinely happy to hear from him. "How are you?"

"I'm doing good, real good." I heard joy in his voice. "As you know, I'm no longer with Blare."

"No, I didn't know," I said. "I'm not at that office anymore either." I was eager to know what he was doing. "What are you up to now?"

"Well, a few things lined up for me when I started temping at an architectural firm," Jason said. "One day, I brought in some of my designs from college—"

"College?" I said, instead of just thinking it as I intended.

"Yeah, college," he answered. "I never finished though."

"Sorry." I frowned, wishing I hadn't let it slip.

"They were so impressed that while I'm working for them in the office, they're paying to develop my skills by sending me to a technical school to get the proper licenses to start me on my way as an architect." I could sense Jason smiling. "Things couldn't be better. I got a nice apartment, a phone, as you can tell, I was able to get a car, too, nothing fancy, but it gets me to and fro, ya know?"

"I'm so happy for you, Jason," I said. "Wow, I truly hope that this is exactly what you need."

"Man, I'm so excited about finally having the chance to be an architect," he said. "My dream."

"I know your mom must be proud," I said.

"Oh, yeah," he said. "But she didn't like that I had to move so far."

"Where are you?" I asked.

"In Joliet, but she acts like I'm in California somewhere." He laughed.

"Wait." I had to confirm. "You're in Joliet?" I asked.

"Yep," he replied. "The school is up here."

"Wow." I giggled. "I'm in Joliet too."

"Get the hell outta here," he said. "Are you serious?"

I was in disbelief as I answered, "Yes. I moved up here to work at the new Blare location they built."

"Wow." He paused. "You know what this means, right?"

"No. What?" I asked.

"It means that you'll have to let me make that awful night up to you." He continued, correcting himself, "No, it means that I *will* make that awful night up to you."

"You don't owe me anything, Jason. I had a great time that night," I said.

"If you say so, but I think I was an asshole." He said it, I didn't. "I was going through a lot of drama back then, but there was something that kept drawing me to you, and I wanted to be around you even if I didn't have shit to offer you."

"Oh, you showed me what you had to offer," I joked.

"Ah, man." He laughed. "I was hoping you didn't remember that."

"How could I ever forget that thing?" I said loudly. "I guess you showed half the office. I see a few ladies got the same flowers I did."

"Huh?" he asked. "Who?"

"Lesley and Denise." Why was I questioning this man's dealings? "I mean, you don't owe me an explanation or anything."

"Lesley is my daughter's grand-aunt. The flowers are for her to take to my baby girl. And Denise, c'mon, man, I know you couldn't think anything about Denise!" He laughed. "I gave Denise flowers because she asked me to bring some for her after she saw me with yours. She wanted to plant them at home."

"Oh," I said. "Well, I thought if you took it out for me, you had taken it out for everyone."

"Well, honestly and unfortunately, back then, that was the only thing I had to offer you." Jason spoke from the heart. "I have so much more to offer you," he hinted. "But I don't know if you'd let me."

"Let you what?" I asked.

"Take you out." He pushed the envelope. "What are you doing this evening?"

"Are you serious?" I answered.

"Yeah," he said. "Are you free?"

"Yes," I said.

Jason said, "Well, not anymore."

"Just like that?" I asked.

"Yep, just like that," he said.

That evening, we met at the Texas Roadhouse on Tonti Drive. It wasn't five-star dining, but it was what he was willing to offer me, which was more than he had before. Jason looked like a new man. He even had a different swag about him, very dapper and un-thuggish, smelling like a man I could hold for days. He even spoke differently. I guess he was really seizing the moment. I was happy for him, and hoped that I would be close to watch him go far.

Jason commented on my weight loss and seemed transfixed on me the entire night. While it was great to feel wanted again, this time, I wasn't desperate for attention anymore. It didn't matter what people thought about me, it was what I felt about me that mattered. Self-love is the soil and love from another is a seed. If my soil isn't in optimum condition, then nothing that is planted there will flourish. My new attitude had nothing to do with me being thinner. I had started living for me, and not for the opinion of others. I now walked out on stage naked, leaving behind the smoke and mirrors.

ORDER FORM
URBAN BOOKS, LLC
78 E. Industry Ct
Deer Park, NY 11729

Name: (please print): _____

Address: _____

City/State: _____

Zip: _____

QTY	TITLES	PRICE
	16 ½ On The Block	$14.95
	16 On The Block	$14.95
	Betrayal	$14.95
	Both Sides Of The Fence	$14.95
	Cheesecake And Teardrops	$14.95
	Denim Diaries	$14.95
	Happily Ever Now	$14.95
	Hell Has No Fury	$14.95
	If It Isn't love	$14.95
	Last Breath	$14.95
	Loving Dasia	$14.95
	Say It Ain't So	$14.95

Shipping and handling - add $3.50 for 1st book, then $1.75 for each additional book.
Please send a check payable to:
Urban Books, LLC
Please allow 4 - 6 weeks for delivery

ORDER FORM
URBAN BOOKS, LLC
78 E. Industry Ct
Deer Park, NY 11729

Name: (please print): _____

Address: _____

City/State: _____

Zip: _____

QTY	TITLES	PRICE
	The Cartel	$14.95
	The Cartel#2	$14.95
	The Dopeman's Wife	$14.95
	The Prada Plan	$14.95
	Gunz And Roses	$14.95
	Snow White	$14.95
	A Pimp's Life	$14.95
	Hush	$14.95
	Little Black Girl Lost 1	$14.95
	Little Black Girl Lost 2	$14.95
	Little Black Girl Lost 3	$14.95
	Little Black Girl Lost 4	$14.95

Shipping and handling - add $3.50 for 1st book, then $1.75 for each additional book.

Please send a check payable to:

Urban Books, LLC

Please allow 4 - 6 weeks for delivery

ORDER FORM
URBAN BOOKS, LLC
78 E. Industry Ct
Deer Park, NY 11729

Name: (please print): _____

Address: _____

City/State: _____

Zip: _____

QTY	TITLES	PRICE
	A Man's Worth	$14.95
	Abundant Rain	$14.95
	Battle Of Jericho	$14.95
	By The Grace Of God	$14.95
	Dance Into Destiny	$14.95
	Divorcing The Devil	$14.95
	Forsaken	$14.95
	Grace And Mercy	$14.95
	Guilty & Not Guilty Of Love	$14.95
	His Woman, His Wife His Widow	$14.95
	Illusions	$14.95
	The LoveChild	$14.95

Shipping and handling - add $3.50 for 1st book, then $1.75 for each additional book.

Please send a check payable to:

Urban Books, LLC

Please allow 4 - 6 weeks for delivery

ORDER FORM
URBAN BOOKS, LLC
78 E. Industry Ct
Deer Park, NY 11729

Name: (please print):_____

Address: _____

City/State: _____

Zip: _____

QTY	TITLES	PRICE

Shipping and handling - add $3.50 for 1st book, then $1.75 for each additional book.
Please send a check payable to:
    Urban Books, LLC
Please allow 4 - 6 weeks for delivery